A Psychology of Insects

Serge Anatole Fedorowsky

A Psychology of Insects

Sorcerer's Way Press

PART I:

PUSHING THE STATIC

Chapter One

It was absolutely beyond his control, welling in his chest and humming up his throat like summer wasps in a small glass jar. Standing in the narrow green doorway to his apartment, mail scattered on the front step, Henry clinched his latest quarterly evaluation tightly around the edges of the smooth cheap paper. The drone hovered at chest height, fruitlessly waiting for him to move.

As he added and subtracted the rows again, the drone let off a quiet ding and echoed out a short pre-recorded message asking him to scan his ID for confirmation of delivery. In his shock, Henry had forgotten the machine existed, the gentle chopping of its swirling blades blending in with the cars and rails and adverts for new ways to raise your personal improvement score that formed the background layer of noise in the small closed off courtyard below. He held out his wrist and let the drone scan the chip that had been placed just above his radial artery on his sixteenth birthday. The pale green light washed over his arm and the drone emitted a low, crackling buzz that grated at the ears before flying off.

"Are you alright, neighbor?" Asked a voice from Henry's left. A short man with a sharp, pointed jaw hovered in his doorway, adjusting the collar on his blue sweater.

"I'm fine, thanks for asking."

"Just checking in to make sure my neighbor is okay. You'll let me know if something is wrong, won't you?"

Henry looked up at the 360 degree camera placed in the center of the courtyard and back at the stranger he was discovering to be his neighbor.

"I will." He responded flatly. "Thank you for being a great neighbor."

A wave of relief washed over the stranger's face as he extended his thumb up towards Henry.

"Anytime." The man said, turning his body away from the courtyard and ducking into his doorway.

Henry stood in his door for a moment longer, thinking about his score and what had happened in the past five minutes. He tried to put a number on the damage he had done to his report by delaying the delivery, and whether the points would come out of social consciousness, order and peace, or some combination of categories that he could not fathom at that moment. He slowly gathered his mail from the ground, making a show of picking up every last piece before returning to his room. He would not be losing points for littering, no matter how the day had started.

Inside his thin studio apartment, Henry pressed himself up against the cold concrete wall in order to pass around the edge of his bed and look in the mirror. He started at himself hard, locking eyes with his reflection as best he could, switching from one eye to the other and questioning why it was impossible to look into both eyes of a reflection at the same time. The darting blue eyes staring back at him were somber. His long, wide nose and thick brown hair did not seem less attractive than they had last quarter, and yet he had managed to drop three whole points in physical appearance. This man looked healthy to Henry, a good weight, a good face, a good-enough sense of fashion that should have given him the edge to stay out of the negatives. For the first time in years, Henry felt a sickly feeling spreading from the pit of his stomach. It oozed through his blood and pumped through his body, his heart carrying it to the very tips of his fingers and toes, infecting him wholly and without compromise.

He wanted to scream again, to grab the mirror and smash it into tiny dust shards that he could take in his hands and inhale deeply. He wanted to tear down the poster of the travel zones he had hanging on his wall for motivation and rip it into pieces so small they could float in the hot dry air of his concrete apartment. He wanted to burst through the wall and shake his unknown neighbor so hard his skeleton would liquify, melting onto the floor for only bothering to go through the performance of caring as the cameras focused in.

Henry could not scream, though. Instead, he sat quietly at the edge of his bed, staring at the postcard of Mt. Sopris he had propped against his nightstand. The image of the snowy peaks dotted with pine trees and honest to god elk roaming the untouched wild seemed infinitely removed from his stifling apartment at that moment. The strata symbol of one hundred points in the corner seemed to rise out against the blue sky, blocking him from even imagining himself there.

Without his looks to save him, Henry wondered how many more quarters he would have to wait to break into the upper-strata. Still clutching his report in his left hand, he tried to imagine where he could squeeze in the extra points to pull himself up. Sponsored viewing stuck out to him. Just a few documentaries a week could push him up a point, but even that seemed too difficult at the moment. He tried to imagine the new slate of films on corporate advances in synthetic fabrics and retched.

The clock embedded in his wall dinged like it had finished baking him for the morning. Henry sighed and took one last look at the postcard's sweeping vista before reaching out and flipping it over. He grabbed a breakfast bar and an overcoat to brave the dry December weather that had settled in on the Metropol before slipping on his shoes and setting his mind on work. As he reached the door the lights shut themselves off, leaving only the blinking red camera eye perched at the corner of his room to flicker in the dark, watching to make sure everything would remain safe.

Chapter Two

It was drafty in the Number 12 Rail Station, the wind cutting under the concrete overhangs and whistling across the dimpled surfaces of the shallow benches that dotted the cold, smooth floors. On average, it took Henry twice as long to get to work by rail, but after his morning had unfolded so abruptly he felt uneven, as if everything he could see was tilted off to one side. The thought of driving on the slanted, curving highway seemed dangerous, his stomach turning in knots as he imagined navigating the compact cluster of sliding cars. Access to the express lane had been a great motivator for his morning commute, and now that it was out of reach it seemed strange and foolish to Henry. He wondered to himself why cars needed to exist in a city where the rail spread out like purple veins just below the skin. His mind lingered on the patterns of the railway map before switching abruptly to the station, the noise of the morning commuters cutting in abruptly like a radio being turned on in another room.

The elevated rail looked down over the tightly packed streets of the Metropol, weaving above them like a slow river. Everything down below seemed to stack on top of itself, the people stepping up and over each other in waves and the buildings stacking, rising story by story one on top of the other far up into the sky. Even from the station platform three stories above the street, the bulk of the Metropol seemed up above Henry's head floating in the clouds. Henry rubbed the back of his neck and tried to look straight ahead, but found himself continuing to drift up, as if some unknown power was pulling on thin wires weaved into his pupils, the microscopic thread sewn in as snugly as one of the buttons in his immaculate brown suit.

On the other end of the platform a thin, skeletal man with a smoke-stained beard and milky eyes stood reciting poetry to a crowd of half-interested commuters in a voice that reminded Henry of a car failing to turn over. Henry watched the people tune in and out as they checked their watches and looked for the train to arrive, barely picking up the ending to the poem.

"I am here!"
a man called to the stars,
his arms open wide enough
to catch the light
dripping from the moon.

As he awaited a reply,
he felt altogether small,
and so he left the stars
to dangle on their
fragile threads,
turning toward
the cicada earth
to bury himself
in the mud.

The crowd surrounding the man murmured to themselves before announcing their opinions loud enough for the speakers to record them. All variations on a theme of "Nicely read" or "Artistic" or "valuable" designed to keep the old beggar from defaulting on his credit.

"Too long". A man in a sharp gray suit called out above the chattering.

The train pulled in and the morning commuters filled the station, diluting the crowd and shuffling the population until it was a new crowd entirely. The old man began to recite another poem, his pale gaze tilting up, crossing threads with the entire rushing population.

Henry stepped into the car of the 12 Rail as the doors closed and found an empty seat by the door next to a woman who leaned up against the window sleeping. The video display reminded the passengers to practice courtesy before picking up speed with gentle precision. Henry watched half-heartedly as the display that lined the walls of the train faded into the image of a man sitting in a small three-legged chair on a dark soundstage. Looking around the rail car, he watched all the men in gray suits staring at the walls.

"Hello, and welcome. I won't waste much of your time today, just a brief description. For your edification, a musical treat from the distant past: foreigners composing Western music. Here, the Mandala Symphony from Toshiro Mayazumi. Remember to save your opinions for the break, and please stay seated."

The car erupted in a cacophonous sound that pushed Henry's heels into the ground. The air felt dense and compact, and Henry found himself grinding his teeth to the vibrations in the air before opening his molars up and keeping them from touching. He couldn't afford a poor health score by wearing down the enamel on his teeth. In the minutes that followed, passengers nodded and smiled to themselves, or grimaced and coughed to indicate their reaction to the music. The man on the monitor sat perfectly still in his chair, save for his fingers, which seemed to be tapping to some unknown pattern only he could identify in the sound.

When the piece had reached a natural stopping point and the 12 Rail rolled into the next station people leaned into the small microphones on their seats and spoke their opinions softly before scanning their wrists to ensure their opinions were properly recorded. The woman slumped over next to Henry sat up and leaned in close to her microphone, pushing the air densely between her peach-pink lips and the listening station.

"It's like you're trying to crush me into a diamond." She whispered, a smile barely managing to emerge from the corner of her mouth.

The woman leaned back and let the station beep as it waited for her to scan her ID, closing her eyes and ignoring its persistent request as the train finished its slow, measured stop. When the doors opened, the woman stood with purpose, stepping over Henry and exiting the train. Henry watched her pass by the rail through the window, his eyes tracing the outline of the design on her black jacket, a small lemon tree and the words "Jade Mountain Teahouse" embroidered in golden thread.

As Henry stepped off the 12 Rail, the door almost closing in on him, he realized he hadn't left a comment. He tried to imagine what he would have said as he descended the stairs to the sidewalk below, but nothing came to mind. As he weaved his way through the crowd to work, he wondered how not leaving a comment would affect his credit. He was tired of caring how each little thing he did would pay dividends down the road, and he was tired of worrying about how his present actions might rob his future self of some small comfort. He spent his free time feeling like a thief, or looking back at his past self, set aglow in a soft lens that made it easy to hate himself.

He imagined his past self huffing glass dust and smiled at the very corners of his lips before snapping himself back to the large concrete facade that housed the Department of Records and Retention. He paused and checked his watch, waiting until the exact moment the clock struck nine to scan his wrist and enter the building. It was important, he thought, to establish intent in timing, to make sure they knew that whatever happened, he had arrived at the exact time he wanted to arrive. To make sure everyone knew that he was in complete control of his life.

"Better to be intentionally on time then accidentally early." he said aloud, believing he was only speaking to himself.

Chapter Three

Inside the offices of the Department of Records and Retention, Henry's heels clicked across the cool marble floor, echoing through the deserted hallway. As he walked, his eyes scanned the executive doorways that lined the long path around the inside perimeter of the building, each one granting more immediate access to work. Of all the benefits of moving upstrata, this was the only one that seemed a disadvantage to Henry. He enjoyed the walk around the empty halls, the thought of dust settling in the wake of every step, covering up his tracks. The feeling of being invisible and forgotten.

The sound of his shoes echoing through the halls built up in the distance and rolled back toward Henry, each step he had taken since he entered the building playing back on delay. It reminded Henry of looking over old photos of unpleasant memories, feelings coming back in muted tones, the images fading in color and emotion in equal proportions with time.

As he arrived at the door to the processing floor, he wanted to look back and yell into the past, to say something that would sound soothing as it faded in the distance. If he could have put a word or name to what was bothering him at that exact moment he would have screamed it just to hear it disappear, but he could not describe the feeling that had begun to roost between his ribcage. The only way he could describe it was something like a bird, an old magpie living out its final, bitter days from the safety of his chest. Henry whispered the word "magpie" to himself before passing through the wide doors to the central processing room and making his way to desk #104.

Everything was laid out immaculately from the Sabbath, his pens and notepads looking better rested and more ready for work than ever. In the middle of his desk, next to a tall stack of documents waiting to be sent to their proper destination was a small piece of folded paper with his name on it. Henry had never received anything like this before, but he knew what was inside. Henry unfolded the summons quickly and read the note to himself.

"Please see me at 9am." His lips moved along with the note before checking the clock on the wall and stuffing the paper into his jacket pocket. It was already ten past nine.

"Good Sabbath?" Jane asked from her seat as Henry rushed by, apologizing loosely for not having the time to talk before hurrying up the winding metal staircase that stood in the center of the room.

As he arrived in the foyer on the second floor, Henry turned to observe the four unmarked doors, each with an assistant sitting at a desk, guarding them. Standing in the middle of the room, he could feel the eight eyes watching him.

"Supervisory?" Henry asked all the assistants at once, spinning in a circle.

Three of the assistants pointed at a young woman with her hand raised just above her shoulder. Henry hastily grabbed for the note, struggling to remove it from his pocket before asking to speak with his supervisor.

"You're late." the woman said, her gray eyes falling from his face to the note.

"I start work at 9 am." He replied.

"Your meeting was at 9." She said looking back at him.

"I think they'd still want to see me."

The assistant grimaced slightly and made a face that conveyed nothing more to Henry than the realization that, regardless of what happened, she had nothing to gain from talking to him.

"You can have a seat." She said, waving her hand toward the other end of the room.

Henry looked around, but found no chairs or stools, just marble flooring and four people watching him with intent. It felt as if they were waiting for him to sit, as if their ability to do their jobs depended on him curling onto the floor. Henry crossed his legs and lowered himself onto the ground, watching as the receptionists continued their work.

The clock embedded in the wall above the supervisory receptionist clicked on the second, sending a small shockwave through the air that caused the corner of her mouth to twitch ever so slightly. Occasionally, she would place her fingers on her lips, unconsciously aware of the wind-up tick, trying to quiet her nervous habit, but it never worked for more than a moment. It was 9:25 when she finally looked back at Henry, calling his name and inviting him into the supervisory room.

The day had neither started nor proceeded according to form, and as he thanked the receptionist, her eyes barely registering his existence, he had the inescapable suspicion that things would not level out.

Chapter Four

As the door closed behind him, Henry froze inside the long, narrow office, his eyes unable to find a focal point to anchor him to the room. The walls were a shade of white so clear and bright they seemed to be saying something, though as his vision faded in and out, he could not guess what the message was. There was no desk, no windows, and no furniture save for the picture frames, cream frames hung in even increments along the wall, all containing the stucco cream picture, abstract textures that faded into the background. It was a room desperate for something to fill it, he thought, as he stepped across the freshly cleaned floor. It demanded a person to take up space and give it purpose. The image of a fly caught in a glass jar rang through Henry's head with the clarity of a tuning fork.

"You're late." A young woman called out from behind him.

Henry spun around to face the voice, his eyes locking intensely on her flowing blue top. She seemed to appear from the walls or floor, stepping through a crack too small to be perceived by normal people.

"I clocked in at 9." He replied, trying to move his eyes up from the smooth fabric of her blouse.

She shook her head and bit the inside of her cheek, letting a palpable silence press down on his shoulders.

"You mustn't put up these barricades. When you defend yourself, you look awfully guilty."

"Guilty?" Henry said, the word falling out of the back of his throat in a whisper.

"Our meeting was at 9, and you kept me waiting." She said, crossing her arms and resting her index finger on her lower lip. "It's impossible to predict how this will affect my day, but you should hope it does not bring any misfortune."

Henry wanted to apologize, but as he ran his gaze over her glossy eyes, something in his chest pulled his words down, catching them in the base of his throat. The bird in his chest had grabbed them, pulling them like a crow pulls at worms in the ground. The woman paced the room toward him, weaving back and forth on the floor, her black heels clicking like marbles dropped from the top floor of a tall building. He tried to pull his eyes away from her tight beige pants, but he couldn't stop comparing them to the color of the walls.

"This," she said, stopping inches from him, "is about your performance."

As she stopped, her scent continued ahead of her, small white flowers in clear spring water, the kind of scent that barely leaves a memory, just an imprint of clean, pure air.

"In what way?" He responded, raising his eyes to meet her gaze. As their eyes locked, the emptiness of the room took on a new weight, her undistracted gaze squeezing in on him from all sides and causing his palms to sweat.

"In the way you perform your job." She said, rolling her eyes slightly. "Tell me, what do you do on a daily basis?"

His pre-arranged answer dripped from the roof of his mouth.

"I copy records requests and redirect information to its proper department."

"And in the four years I've managed you, you've done a fine job of that. Mostly, anyways."

Henry tried to recall whether this woman had been his supervisor for the past four years. He had never seen her before, and as he tried to recall his last meeting with his supervisor, no such interaction came to mind.

"But," she continued, "three requests directed to the parks department that lacked BSR approval in the past year looks bad no matter how well you keep your head down."

Henry failed to grasp what was happening, her words sliding off of him and collecting at his feet.

"The Bureau of Social Responsibility needs to approve all quality-of-life adjustments. It's in the handbook. You have read it, I assume?"

"Page 3, *Requests of Basic Adjustments.*"

"Improvements to Sub-Strata green space, Improvements to Defaulter Park Space, Restratification of Northwest Park and Zoo? These hardly seem like Parks Department decisions, do they?"

His words caught up in his throat again as he fumbled to grasp when this had happened.

"You'll be docked a point for Work Productivity next quarter, and another if this happens again. Do you understand?"

"Yes." He said, the autopilot of his work day playing back in his mind, the mistakes popping into focus slowly.

"Now please, stop staring at me and get out."

Henry's skin flushed and his eyes snapped shut as he caught them drifting down to her shoes. He breathed deeply and held the air in for a long time before opening his eyes to an empty, formless room.

Back on the processing floor, he leaned back in his chair, convincing himself to start the day.

"Did you break 100?" Jane asked from her desk, smiling in a way that told Henry she knew the answer.

"99 again."

"And a meeting? Looks like someone's starting to slip."

"I'm not slipping."

Her eyes sank slightly around the edges, and her tone softened as she leaned in close to him.

"It's always hard to tell when it's happening, but that's why I'm bringing it up. You need to address it early."

"I'm not sliding. It's just this quarter."

"What was it? Friendliness?"

"No."

"You have been kind of mean lately."

"It was Physical Appearance."

Jane pursed her lips to stifle a noise that Henry suspected was laughter.

"Well it's not so bad. It's probably just your suit and hair." She said, holding up a piece of paper and dividing him into easy to digest pieces.

"What's wrong with the suit?"

"It's maybe a little... brown, I guess."

Henry looked around the office for other brown suits, but found none.

"And the hair?"

"Your hair is fine." Jane said, turning her attention back to her desk.

"You just mentioned my hair."

"I don't think I did."

Jane turned to him and smiled, taking a sip from her coffee in a way that displayed the photo of her on Mt. Sopris that she had printed on the side of her mug. As helpful as she could be, Henry had learned to recognize the subtle pressure that his coworker exuded, the relentless signals she sent into the world to let others know exactly where she stood on the social ladder, and he had grown to truly dislike her for it.

Henry smiled back at her and nodded before turning his mind to work and the large stack of file requests that had piled up on the edge of his desk in his absence. As he flipped through the maps and charts that the Parks Department had requested, his eyes rested on the wilderness zone at the edge of the Fuel Yards. His mind wandered to the hills that sat just out of sight from the Metrapol's tallest vista, to the streams and trees that had populated his waking thoughts for the past three years, barely registering his daily work. He spent the rest of the afternoon drifting in and out of a dream: standing on a riverbank, watching water fall through the yawning mouth of an infinite cave. A world as obscure as a pure white room without a focal point.

Chapter Five

After work Henry walked the lower levels of the city, his mind floating over his body like a balloon on a long string trailing behind him. The sun was well past the midday point that allowed light to penetrate into the street, leaving the faux-neon LEDs to cast shadows in tinted shades of purple and blue across the sidewalks. Passing by a long empty window, Henry stopped to examine himself beneath the flickering yellow light of a nightclub marquee that made his suit look orange and sick.

He walked up and down the streets in blocks, circling one before expanding in larger concentric circles, his eyes washing over everything in a half-interested glaze. He felt as though he was watching himself pace out a maze, stamping it into the ground beneath his slow mechanical feet. Jane's comment stuck in his floating brain and rattled around, the thought of slipping down the social ladder unable to shake loose. He imagined himself struggling to stay afloat, watching his score slip away quarter after quarter, every damage tacking on and pulling him down into the depths of society until he couldn't breathe. Henry's body gasped, trapping air just below his throat and swallowing it, his brain barely bothering to regulate the shell it had come to control.

As his mind wandered, his feet began to turn slowly, one over the other like a train coming into the station until he was barely moving at all. His brain continued to float on ahead of him, wandering further and further from his form as it came glued to its spot beneath the yellow-green neon, floating off into the quiet sunset streets. Slowly his mind began to forget his form, as it continued out west through the occasional echo of hard rubber soles on concrete, ratcheting up through the canyon of buildings, until there was no memory of who or what he once was.

When Henry's body snapped itself out of its still trance, he felt like a traveler returning to his long neglected home, the memories of far and exotic places still haunting his silent moments. As he began to feel the familiarity in his surroundings, Henry let out the last breath of stale air he had been holding in his lungs since the morning report came in. Breathing in, he could have sworn his lungs went on forever, a small hole leaking air out of his back or side into the cooling night.

The blinking neon lemon above the Jade Mountain Teahouse shined down and melted into his skin, defusing a pleasant lemon aroma deep in his core. It was well past nine o'clock, and the lemon-scent that leaked from Henry's pores made him salivate. He looked around for any sign of a diner or quick-cafe before stepping into the teahouse, pushing the red and black door open with a soft touch of his fingers.

Inside, the sound of a stray trumpet wafted down from the second-story balcony. The projected image of a young man with an incredibly square jaw sat at a bar stool playing soft, distant melodies. The teahouse was almost deserted, a few men at a corner table and a couple on the balcony, studying the image as it began to sing "Let's Get Lost".

"Can I help you?" a maître d' asked, stepping out from the seating floor and coughing into his own throat.

Henry asked the pale, damp looking man for a seat by the bar, and was escorted past two men arguing fiercely under their breath about work. Everything in the teahouse seemed subdued, from the red and gold carpet to the soft pale light that sunk into the low oak tables. Even the volume seemed to be turned down, the music drifting from the balcony as if it were taking place behind a thin pane of perfectly clear glass. At the bar, Henry watched the trumpet player closely, unsure if the smooth eyes and limbs actually belonged to a projection at all. He felt a hand run down his forearm, turning to find the woman from his morning train holding a scanner up to the chip in his wrist, her jet black hair cutting a stark outline against the soft-lit bar. She pursed her peach-pink lips slightly as she reviewed the results on a screen behind the counter.

"You haven't been here before." She said, holding up a blank electronic menu.

"I was just walking by. Sorry." He said, not needing any explanation to know what she meant.

Henry stood to leave, but the woman's hand stayed gently stuck to his wrist. Standing halfway between the bar and the tables, he turned to look at her, their eyes locking into place together. She pulled him back gently, her hands barely moving, a mere suggestion that he should return to his seat.

Henry knew he shouldn't, but there was something in her movement that was decisive, commanding even. She placed an empty glass tea cup in front of him and poured an almost transparent brown tea.

"Puher, Old Sri Lanka, Traditional." She said, pushing the cup towards Henry and insisting he try it as she finally released his arm.

He blew on the hot cup and took a sip, his eyes expanding in their sockets as he let the liquid slide across his tongue into his throat.

"Is this real tea?" He asked under his breath.

"Puher, Old Sri Lanka, Traditional." She repeated.

He took another sip and let the subtle flowers of fruit and something new and earthy he had never tasted wash over his palette.

"I shouldn't be drinking this." He said, warming his hands on the cup.

"Is it bad?"

"No. I'm..." Henry slid his wrist up and placed it on the hot cup, letting it burn him slightly.

"One point off of up-strata? That seems close enough."

Henry's face was a blank mask. He had never considered that being close to reaching his goals could net him any reward. His mind rearranged the neurons in his head like a Rubik's Cube, forming new connections for an alien concept.

"You could get in trouble."

"Only if you tell." She held a swizzle stick up and pointed it at the corners of the room, sending Henry's eyes turning in search of some hidden code. He examined the walls for some time before returning a result like a slow computer.

"Cameras?" He asked.

"In a cafe beau monde? Not likely."

Henry felt lightning in his chest.

"Listening?"

She gently turned her head from side to side, a soft smile forming at the edge of her lips.

"You can relax." She said, pointing her swizzle stick wand at his tea, a spell that made him pick up the glass and drink.

The two sat in silence as Henry drank, his mouth almost forming words again and again as he processed his surroundings.

"If no one is watching, then..." The question couldn't form itself, at least not entirely. No matter how hard he tried, it stayed imperfect, single words popping in and out of his head, a feeling forming in his chest like an unhatched egg waiting to crack.

"I'm Eva." She said, studying his face.

Henry didn't respond, he just watched her as she slipped out from behind the bar and poured tea in the glasses of the two men arguing behind him. One of the men, whose tight ponytail looked as though it was holding his skin in place, looked at Henry with a deep questioning stare. Henry gripped his teacup as if it were the only floating thing in the sea as he imagined the man's ponytail coming loose, skin sliding down from his face.

Eva returned and refilled his cup.

"I saw you on the rail this morning." Henry said.

"Oh? Which stop?"

"Number 12 Rail Station. You didn't scan your wrist at the terminal."

She put the swizzle stick between her teeth and bit off a tiny crystal.

"They wouldn't have liked my response."

"Crushed like a diamond…" Henry said, staring at the rock candy.

Eva smiled. "Don't you ever feel that way?" she asked.

Henry nodded his head slowly, his eyes drifting down to his tea.

"Better to not leave a response at all than to leave anonymous feedback. Score-wise, I mean."

"That's a theory, I suppose." She said, her fingers grazing the edge of a fresh teacup. A silence lingered between the two before she looked up, popping the long pause like a bubble. "How much do you know about money?" She asked suddenly.

Henry looked over his shoulder at the man in the ponytail, the two making short eye contact.

"Not much. It was a third good that people used for trade."

"You could exchange it for anything if you had enough of it. Isn't that funny? Anything at all."

"It was prone to defacing, though, and people could hold on to it and stop it from circulating."

"You read that, or hear it?"

Henry began to tense up from his feet.

"Why did you bring it up?" He asked with a cautious smile.

"No reason, really. If you had money, you could buy this tea whenever you wanted. You could kill a man, walk into a cafe, and buy tea before they had time to arrest you."

"I wouldn't kill someone."

"There aren't any cameras here."

"I wouldn't kill anyone."

"No microphones, either."

"Well I still wouldn't do that."

Eva's eyes folded slightly at the edges, unraveling Henry like a spool of brown thread.

"If you had money, nothing could stand between you and what you wanted except that money. You wouldn't have to be nice, or good, or current. You would just need money."

"The history of money is the history of people building prisons for themselves." Henry said, looking into his tea. "There's never enough, it's always scarce, so you push until you have the means to borrow, and then you can't stop collecting it or everything falls apart. Before long, you've built yourself a cage, locked yourself into a number you need, and no amount of smashing will break those bars. It's just people inventing scarcity to control each other. It always ends violently."

An arm wrapped around Henry's shoulder, locking him into the chest of a stranger.

"What the kid doesn't understand is it ends in violence either way. Isn't that right?" The man in the ponytail said, looking at Eva and showing a thin-lipped grin.

Henry pushed against the man, but couldn't get free.

"Let him go." Eva said calmly, a smile escaping her lips.

The man loosened his arm, letting Henry slip free, almost tumbling out of his chair onto his feet. He backed away from the bar, watching Eva speak with the man, her eyes unaware of his steady retreat toward the exit. As he approached the door, the sick, wet maître d' grabbed him by the arm and slipped a card into his breast pocket.

"Do come back again, should you want to speak further."

Henry slipped out into the streets and found himself running down the nearest alley. He wanted air, but all he could find was the stale smell of heat radiating off the cooling concrete. Leaning against a steel wall, he tried to stop the feeling of something reaching up from his stomach, catching his air and stopping him from exhaling.

It was then that he noticed a small man sitting in a box, his tattered brown suit and graying hair triggering a feeling of vertigo, of looking down at himself from the industrial high wires of the city above. They didn't speak or stay together, but in that moment, Henry realized the grim fact that once all of the day's odd transgressions were added up, he would be sliding. Officially, without a doubt, sliding, his entire life crumbling away from him like skin peeling off strip by strip.

Henry collected himself and made his way to the rail without a single thought coming into focus. He was on autopilot, a husk trying to keep its form, the season's last cicada shell resting on a cool black bough. The rail whistled into the station and Henry stepped aboard, the whole of his life ready for processing in the coming hours.

Chapter Six

Arriving at the courtyard of the Brittany Manor Apartments, Henry paused for a moment to drink in the cool night air. Everything was charged with static, the tree branches and faux flowers that dotted the inner gate live and shaking, as if a hundred strangers had been wandering the space mere seconds before he arrived. Henry ran his hands through the outlines of people stitched into the aether, pushing the static aside and scattering it into the evening.

His feet turned over the steps as he made his way to the fifth floor, one over the other, in a way that made him feel as though he was getting nowhere at all. Looking up the staircase, he always felt the same distance from his goals, like he would never make it off of the rattling metal steps. Some imperceptible force, god maybe, building new steps above him and removing the ones beneath him until he was wandering up through the stratosphere, into space, unable to go anywhere or do anything but move one foot over the other.

When Henry realized he had reached his narrow door he pulled himself out of the trance and turned the handle. The lights were already on inside, his supervisor sitting on the edge of his bed, flipping through his unused postcards. She yawned as he entered, covering her mouth with a postcard of the Pacific Ocean and crossing her legs. Henry peeked behind the door to see if there was anyone else inside.

"How mousy of you." She said, tossing his postcard across the bed. "We're alone."

Henry stepped inside cautiously, leaving the door open behind him.

"How can I help you?" He asked, his voice cracking slightly.

"You don't have to be so polite. I had your camera disabled."

A shot of cold poison coursed through Henry's left arm as his eyes shot toward his camera, the light no longer blinking.

"Won't I get in trouble for that?"

"And how. It would have been worth it if you got here sooner, but now you'll just be in trouble."

His supervisor stood and undid the belt on her coat, revealing an immaculate set of deep red lingerie that fit tightly against her pale skin. She let the image burn into Henry for a moment before closing the coat.

"How'd you get in here?"

"I told them I was here to inspect your room for illicit materials. As your supervisor, I take my job very seriously."

Henry tried to let all of the information into his head alongside the image of his supervisor undressing. It was like his brain was taking on water, his body throwing information out of his head to keep the image afloat in his mind.

"They're going to think I'm a criminal."

"Just tell them you're not. It might work. Or at least, it probably would if you weren't slipping so badly."

"I have it under control."

The woman sighed, stepping across the room in her red bottom heels and standing too close to make Henry feel anything but an intense discomfort.

"I'll make you a deal. I'll vouch for you, I'll tell them I turned your camera off, say I didn't find anything, and I'm pretty tired, but I'll still sleep with you on one condition. Before anything else happens, I want you to say my name."

Henry opened his mouth to speak, but as he tried to push sound up through his closing throat, nothing came out. He wanted to scream her name and disappear this new nightmare, but as he tried, the stark reality of his situation came clearly into focus. He couldn't say her name because, even with his meeting earlier that day, he did not know it.

"You may be trying to upstrata yourself, but you've been sliding for a long time. You live in a fantasy world where you deserve to get out of this place and see the world, but we both know you're trapped here for a reason. You can't even be bothered to know your supervisor's name, because you think that if you keep your head down and power through you'll make it out on the other side. But what you fail to realize is that if you don't stand out, you'll never be successful. And you just don't stand out."

She stepped past Henry, brushing against him slightly to make certain he felt how soft her hands were.

"My name is Viviana. And believe it or not, I'm trying to help."

She closed the door, trapping Henry inside with his thoughts. There was no one to watch him throw his bedding across the room, no one to listen as he swore at Viviana's static ghost, no one to care about the tears that began to stream down his face as he noticed the light crisp smell of her perfume, fresh cut apples and lilac, lingering over everything. His throat felt raw from a day of clutched panic, and as he screamed into his pillow, he knew his voice would not be here tomorrow.

A knock on the door froze him in his place, kneeling on the floor with a pillow in his hands. He wiped his eyes and pulled his pieces together, hoping that Viviana would be waiting on the other side, ready to fix the mess he was in. As he opened the door, though, he was greeted by his neighbor standing uncomfortably in the cold.

"I heard a lot of noise." He said, standing with his body prone halfway between the doorway and the courtyard camera.

"I'm fine." Henry said softly.

"I wanted to check in."

"I said I'm fine."

The man grimaced slightly at Henry's curt response, not quite getting what he needed.

"Then I wanted to ask you to stop disturbing the peace. A quiet neighbor is a good neighbor."

The two locked eyes, and Henry knew that this man, like him, was not where he wanted to be.

"Are you new here?" Henry asked, donning the same porcelain mask that he had carried on his face that morning.

"No. I've lived here for a year now."

"So why am I just meeting you now?"

The man's nostrils flared and he began to clench and unclench his sharp jaw, his exhale pouring out of his nose like smoke. The neighbor went back to his door, and Henry stared out into the harsh red glow of the courtyard camera. He knew that a technician would be around to fix his camera in the morning, but he had some time before daybreak, and he decided he was going to make the absolute most of it. Inside he locked the door to brace himself from the outside world, taking a bottle of shochu he had been saving to give as a hospitality gift and an energy bar and placing them next to his bed before putting on the most violent, pornographic film he had on physical disc, a copy of *Caligula* he had received from his late father. He stayed up well into the night, drinking to excess, rewinding the film, speaking sentences he knew would undermine his moral credibility if anyone had been listening.

When he was good and drunk, the edges of his vision folding in around him as he swung his head slowly back and forth, he imagined the mountain wind on his face, crisp and cool as he absorbed it into his lungs. Laying back on the mountaintop, he allowed the gentle apple and lilac scented breeze to knock him into a short dreamless sleep from which he did not want to return.

Chapter Seven

Henry woke up when the light was still cold and muted outside, the sound of quick, sudden knocks at his door shocking him into reality. His eyes rattled back and forth as his eyelids shot open like billiard balls after the break, his pupils bouncing around the edges of the room wildly. He rose to his feet softly and made a vain attempt to tidy up before the visitor knocked again, this time twice as loud.

The door opened on two men standing shoulder to shoulder, one with small glasses and a hooked nose in a jumper with the Metrapol Services logo on the chest, the other with long even sideburns in a disassembled suit, his brown sports coat hanging over his shoulder.

"May we?" Asked the man in the sideburns, pulling out a portable scanner and a notepad.

Henry nodded once and the hook-nosed man went straight for the camera, stepping onto the bed to get a better view.

"We've gotten numerous complaints about you this week, and now with the camera, we had to come out." The man in the sideburns said, his eyes drifting over the room behind Henry.

"I understand." Henry said with a smooth, even face.

The camera man said nothing, swiftly taking the camera apart and reassembling it piece by piece in his hands.

"You need to get out of your head. Maybe pick up a hobby. Do you run at all?" The sideburned man said, writing on his notepad.

"Sometimes."

"Maybe go running. There's a track near here. You need to get out of your head." The man yawned and reached into his pocket for a cigarette case, stopping himself and putting it away as he went back to writing. "There's a new show on TV1 about the war. The last one. Sort of a drama. Maybe watch it. You need to get out of your head."

"I understand." Henry said, his voice coming from a distant place in the back of his throat, a black hole where some other Henry lived, separated by time and space.

The man scratched his sideburns with a pen and scanned Henry's wrist before proceeding to the door. The camera man snapped the last pieces into place and set the camera on the wall, returning the blinking red light to its rightful place above Henry's pillow. The light often made its way into Henry's dreams, like the blinking light of a buoy in the distant water, too far to swim towards. He was glad he hadn't dreamt last night, the lack of his constant dreaming companion portending strange newness in his mind. Now, he thought, his mind dissolving the scene playing out in his apartment, he could return to his dreams knowing he was not alone.

"Take the day off and get out of your head, demerit free." The sideburned man said, holding out an official report that identified him as a police officer. "We'll say sick. Go see a friend."

"Thank you." A voice said through Henry.

The officer packed the camera man up like a piece of luggage, placing him at his shoulder as they walked away.

Henry spent the next hour trying to fall back to sleep, but something was stopping him. The loneliness of the room pressed into him, crushing down on his skeleton. He wanted someone to sit with, his mind wandering to Viviana, followed by a still image of Eva smiling at him, her head surrounded by a soft glowing light.

Chapter Eight

It was dark inside the Jade Mountain Teahouse, a few stray lamps illuminating odd corners of the room, propping them up like small islands in a dark sea. Henry felt the raised lettering of the maître d's card against his thumb and floated toward the nearest island, a small wooden table with a deck of cards and a worn copper lamp. Standing on the soft-lit shore, he looked around for Eva, finding only immaculately curated floating worlds.

A fit of muffled coughing cut through the thick liquid dark and drifted out in all directions, filling the room with quiet white noise. The sound collapsed in on itself, dry-drowning or gentle choking drifting around aimlessly until the pale, sweat-laden maître d' stepped into the light.

"Back already." He said, dabbing his forehead with a yellowing cotton cloth. He looked as though he had lost ten pounds since they met the day before.

"I was hoping to speak with Eva."

The maître d' exhaled a long breath from his nose as his eyes sunk down into their sockets. He would have looked disappointed or annoyed, Henry thought, if not for the plaster smile he wore across his lips. It seemed a near perfect replica of an actual smile, detectable only around the very edges of his lips, as if it were hanging across his face from his ears like glasses.

"She didn't show up this morning. You can try later, if you'd like."

Henry tried to think of where he would go to waste time, but the thought of the crowded auto-cafes and diners made his blood crawl. He tried hard to remember when exactly his nerves had gotten so frayed and worn down, but couldn't pinpoint any exact time. It felt new, but as he scanned backwards through time, he could faintly remember a longstanding anxiety swimming just below the surface of his life, as if he were floating through his days on a glass-bottom boat, something many-headed and leviathan barely visible in the dark beneath his feet.

"Are you free to talk?" Henry asked, holding out the card he had been rubbing in his coat pocket.

"That depends on what you'd like to talk about." He said, inhaling deeply and holding it in until his eyes began to water.

"Whatever you want."

The maître d' nodded and waved his cloth-covered hand, stepping back into the dark and reappearing at a table in the back corner next to a painting of a vast desert. Henry stepped into the dark and reappeared at a new island, his mind skipping as he felt the distance between the two collapse down into two small steps. The maître d' snapped his fingers and a young man with perfectly polished skin appeared with a teapot and a single steaming cup, placing them both on the small table. After pouring hot tea into the empty vessel, the maître d' wiped his bald head and leaned in close to inhale the steam that lifted off the porcelain rim. It filtered through his nose and out through his slightly open lips, quieting his cough.

"What did you want to speak to Eva about?" He said, leaving the cup untouched.

Henry turned the question over in his mind without a clear answer.

"She talked about money yesterday. I guess about that."

"Are you a budding Capitalist?" He asked.

"No. But..." Henry thought hard on how to phrase his thoughts. "The lack of barriers is appealing."

"Barriers rarely are appealing." The maître d' said softly.

"It has its advantages, I suppose." Henry said, leaning close across the table hoping to go entirely unheard. Speaking to the maître d' was like speaking to the empty spaces in his dreams.

"Only in so much as any system has its advantages." Said the maître d', moving his hand in an odd circular motion, like shaking up a snow globe. "We live in a world devoid of conflict. This is an advantage, too."

"There's plenty of conflict." Henry replied.

The maître d' scoffed.

"Real, lasting conflict. You cannot go hungry, you cannot go without shelter unless you choose to. The principal guarantee of our society is that so long as you contribute, you will have what you need to survive. That is a great advantage."

Henry pulled his hand back beneath the table.

"So you're not a Capitalist?"

"Non. Were you expecting me to be?"

"I don't know."

"Non, you haven't stumbled on some clandestine club, if that's what you're thinking. Money solves all problems, but at its core it's rotten stuff. You cannot have a system of wealth collection where everyone is able to collect wealth."

"Affluence predetermines poverty." Henry said, thinking back to his days in school.

"The Second Rulebook is not entirely without merit."

"But this..." Henry said, turning the same invisible snow globe in his hand, his words failing him on the cusp of a new idea.

"I suppose that depends on what you think life is, non? If we are here to survive, this is an immaculate construction. We live longer than our ancestors ever did, and there are more of us now than at any point in history."

"Suppose we aren't here to survive."

The maître d' smiled, bending at the waist like a broken robot and inhaling another jet of steam. Henry wanted a drink, but couldn't find the proper time to ask for a cup.

"That's the unknown idea. It isn't Capitalism, or Socialism, or this. It hasn't been invented yet. No system is a monolith, it's a thousand ideas that slowly build up until..." He snapped his fingers sharply. "It appears to form out of thin air."

The two sat in silence as Henry contemplated this. He tried to envision a world where he would be free to go to the mountains, and work, and disappear into the background. A system where he would be truly and radically free. He tried to put the thought to a group, or a place, but the only image that came to mind was a vast and empty plain, a desert stretching infinitely in every direction.

"But in the end, it's not so bad." Continued the maître d'. "All you have to do is live a decent life and things come to you. If you can be a good neighbor, you can live in peace."

"I hate my neighbor."

The maître d' laughed, unlocking his steam seal and letting a cough loose from the bottom of his lungs. He wiped the pale phlegm from his lips with his yellow cloth.

"Then you should learn to love them, or learn to hide." The maître d' stood and made his way across the moving dark to seat a new guest.

Henry reached across the table and took the cup that sat facing him, sipping deeply from it. The hot-sweet mixture burnt his throat slightly, mint and something foreign and earthy lingering on the back of his tongue. It made him feel warm and electric, his breath coming out in tense, choppy segments as he poured himself another cup of tea to indulge his new taste. As Henry sat, steadily draining the teapot, a feeling began to wrap itself around him. It was the same feeling he experienced when the rail came in and he considered throwing himself at the tracks.

As he finished the pot of tea, Henry felt uncontrollably warm inside. His blood was mint and napalm, sticky and thick in his veins. He left the empty pot on the table, placing the cup in his pocket and setting himself on a path toward something terrible.

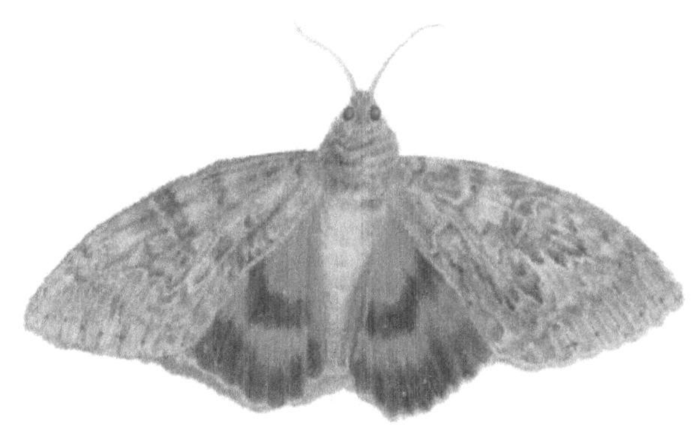# PART II:

STRAWBERRIES AND KEROSINE

Chapter Nine

Detective Gorky sat in front of his computer terminal, staring at an unopened email titled *Code 6*. Reaching into his jacket pocket, he allowed himself a cigarette from a thin silver case, the blinking eye of the Collections Department's central security system trained on his parting lips. Tobacco and Salt singed the hair in his nose and shot wires of blood through his eyes, the capillaries slowly bursting. For a brief moment, he felt as if he could follow the trails forming in his eyes like tree roots, but decided it was a projection brought on by coffee, lost sleep, and strong Salt.

Once the cigarette burnt down to the cotton Gorky opened the email, keeping the butt between his teeth to chew on as he scanned the information:

Henry Chenille; Male; 29; Processor at the Department of Records and Retention.

Erratic behavior beginning at 8:30am, Oct. 22 (Tuesday). Received 15 citations over the following 48 hours, culminating in unauthorized trip to Border Zone 14. No sightings since Oct. 27 (Sunday). Citations include...

Gorky read the citations out loud to himself, trying to put together a string of events that chained each infraction to the next. It was a ritual to him, the understanding that came from reading files again and again, solid groundwork to prepare himself for the chase.

A sound like a pot being dropped struck the walls and bounced around the open office's concrete walls, breaking Gorky's concentration and placing him back at his desk.

Jean-Baptiste grabbed the back of a folding chair and slammed it into the smooth, cold floor in front of him.

"Who put this here?" He waited for a response before throwing the chair on its side and walking to his desk across from Gorky. "Stubbed my damned toe." He laughed, the gaunt angles of his barely shaved face catching shadows beneath his cheekbones.

Gorky spit the cigarette butt into an empty ashtray, his hunched over form staying in its question mark shape a moment longer than he wanted it to, the uncurling of his spine a new and surprising challenge. Jean-Baptiste sniffed the air and smiled, his dull, flat teeth catching the fluorescent light in a way that made it hard to tell which was more yellow.

"Salt?" He asked, picking up the only file on his immaculately clean desk.

"Code 6." Gorky replied, his spine cracking as he reached his full upright posture.

"How easy?"

"He made it to a Border Zone before they lost him."

Jean-Baptiste's eyes crossed back and forth over the file as if he were watching a typewriter.

"Why don't they just get some cops from the outer districts to round him up?"

"Apparently they tried, but it didn't work. He isn't leaving a trail, and they don't know where he's going."

"It's been a while since we've had a proper ghost hunt."

The edges of Gorky's vision widened dramatically as the Salt moved into its second phase, giving him a clear, deep view of the room.

"Where did you go last night?"

Jean-Baptiste shrugged, keeping his eyes on the report. Gorky could only guess what that meant, but something in the dark backroom of his mind told him nothing good had occurred in the past 24 hours. He grimaced and shuffled through the stacks of paper and half opened books that lined his desk, searching for the Chenille file.

"We need to do some legwork before we head for the border." Gorky said, throwing a brown overcoat over his shoulders and looking at his reflection in Jean-Baptiste's unused monitor.

"Let me know when we leave." Jean Baptiste responded, reading the same file for the tenth time.

"You're coming with me."

Jean-Baptiste looked up at Gorky's bloodshot eyes and sighed, putting his hands up in silent protest before grabbing his blue sports coat and slipping it on over his vest. Gorky hated having him along for this part, but he couldn't see it working any other way. There was an energy just below Jean-Baptiste's surface that occasionally oozed out of his pores and dripped out from beneath his fingertips, infecting anything they touched. On the worst days it was as relentless as the rise of the ocean, sending the world around him into a state of panic and despair. It had become a sixth sense to Gorky, knowing when it was at its worst, and everything from the way he stood to the glint in his eye told him that Jean-Baptiste could not be left alone.

As the two gathered their belongings, Gorky looked at Jean-Baptiste's report, a list of allergies, illnesses, and suggestions on how it should be done. Staring at the first suggestion, a small laugh barely escaped the seal of his lips, sending a shock of regret through his system. Gun was an obvious choice, but there was nothing funny about it.

Chapter Ten

The lighting in the municipal library was hard and bright, lending everything it touched a sticky synthetic glow. Detective Gorky adjusted his sunglasses so the frames weren't digging into his temples. They sloped forward, making him look as though he were staring at the librarian's pale green sweater.

"I'm not supposed to show you anyone's records without an order from my supervisor." She said, searching for the detective's eyes, but finding only her reflection, slightly misshapen.

"The 38th amendment gives me the right to request any records as a representative of the government."

She looked at him hesitantly, brushing a stray piece of brown hair from her forehead.

"That applies to records sealed by an individual, not by a third party. I'll need to call my supervisor."

"It's a gray area, but it seems-"

"It seems fairly clear cut to me." She said, placing her hand on the phone and turning to the directory page taped up by the computer.

Gorky tried to contain a smile, but it dripped off his lips. He was used to people folding under pressure, not sure when and where to stand their ground. He reached out his hand to stop her, but Jean-Baptiste beat him to it.

"Clear cut." Jean-Baptiste said, placing his long boney fingers on the receiver to keep it in place. "That's a nice way to put it. Like trees."

Gorky felt his shoulders rolling forward as his muscles began to tighten. The librarian let go of the receiver and grabbed the nearest object her hands could locate, finding a book on Roman tax collection.

"Trees?" She asked softly.

"In the fuel yards they have these machines that swing chains in a circle, round and round and round. They can clear cut an entire forest in a few minutes. All the trees just stand there for a second, like they haven't been cut."

Gorky reached out and tapped him on the shoulder, but Jean-Baptiste swatted his hand away.

"People are like that, too. You could split them in half and most of them wouldn't even know anything was wrong.

"I..." She paused, her words sticky and sharp in her throat, each one a molasses covered burr trying to make its way up her windpipe. "What?"

"I bet you'd notice right away."

"I'm afraid I need to ask you -"

"Don't ask us to leave." Jean-Baptiste said, his tone flattening out into a dead wire. "Cause then we'll have to come back."

Gorky reached out and touched his shoulder again. Jean-Baptiste stood still, letting the hand rest on his shoulder, lingering. The librarian typed a few words on her computer and walked slowly toward the printer, returning with a list of all the books currently checked out to Henry Chenille. Gorky took the list from her shaking hand. He wanted to apologize but couldn't bring himself to do so. As he turned to walk away, Jean-Baptiste lingered a moment longer before turning on his heels and following close behind.

Outside the library the two stood in the cold watching people shuffle in and out of the municipal building.

"Why didn't we just go to the guy's apartment? Why stop at the library?" Jean-Baptiste asked, cleaning his sunglasses.

"No one's going to his apartment, so there's no rush. He visited the library three times in the 48 hours before he ghosted. It feels relevant."

"Well, what's it say?"

Gorky looked at the list and read the titles aloud:

A New-Strata Guide to the Outer Districts

101 Easy Home Dinners

Chinese Naval Shipbuilding: An Ambitious and Uncertain Course

Chapters in the Psychology of Insects

"He's building a boat to sail off into the mountains." Jean-Baptiste said, squinting into the sun before putting on a pair of small round sunglasses that barely covered his eyes.

"Nothing yet. We'll have to wait and see."

"Well maybe we can wait a little faster next time. You would have been talking to her all day."

"I would have gotten the list without traumatizing her." Gorky said.

He carefully folded the list and placed it in his jacket's breast pocket next to his cigarette case.

"She was cute, wasn't she?" Jean-Baptiste asked, smiling and raising one eyebrow.

"You're out of control."

Jean-Baptiste's smile slowly melted off his face, his left upper lip staying slightly raised.

"Who's going to stop me?" He asked, followed by a click of his tongue.

Gorky breathed the cold air deeply, allowing it to freeze him from the inside, the numb, hushed sensation of his body turning crystalline and sharp, stopping him from feeling anything at all. He counted to five in his head, just enough time to transform into an icy shell of his former self.

Chapter 11

Inside the Jade Mountain Teahouse, Detective Gorky waited for someone to greet him. Jean-Baptiste stood just outside the tinted window rocking back and forth on the heels of his freshly polished dress shoes, refusing to come inside. Everyone who passed by the window put a little extra distance between themselves and Jean-Baptiste, walking around lamp posts or hurrying by with their hats down. Gorky imagined a secret chemical coating on his partner's skin, something nobody could see or smell but through thousands of years of evolution had come to sense, like a pressure drop before the rain.

When he turned back, a short bald man stood on the podium sweating through his freshly pressed shirt. The bald man had been staring out the window alongside him, silently cooperating.

"Are you with him?" The man asked, pointing to Jean-Baptiste with a pen and circling him in the window. Jean-

Baptiste squirmed uncomfortably, as if he knew he was being circled.

"He's with me."

Gorky flashed his badge before spiriting it away into his coat, trying not to linger too long on the imbalance of power he had just injected into the conversation.

"It's a pretty badge, but I'm quite sure I'll be no help."

The man circled the spaces where cameras would be with his pen.

"This is recent." Gorky said, adjusting his sunglasses and checking to make sure Jean-Baptiste was still haunting the window. "Yesterday and the day before." He slid a picture of Henry across the podium.

"Yesterday you said?" The maître d' asked, dabbing his pallid skin with an oily yellow rag.

"And the day before."

The maître d' tried to shrug it off, but Gorky could tell from the way his eyes wandered between the window and the doorway that they were on the same page.

"I've been terribly busy this week. I was planning a trip to the lakes, but things haven't gone quite to plan. My mind has been wandering. I don't really know what to do."

Gorky sneered, a sharp pain running up his neck, pulling the skin around his temples tight. He slowly removed his sunglasses, steadying his shaking hand by placing his elbow on the podium as he drew out his cigarette case.

The maître d' smiled, scratching a cigarette out of the case with his thin, sweaty finger and placing it in his pocket. He clapped and looked back toward the bar, the skin glistening on his hands. Gorky imagined dredging a skeleton up from a pot of gravy.

"Why was he here?"

"To see Eva, one of our servers. She wasn't in, though."

"Is she here now?"

The maître d' shifted his focus to the window.

"Do you always make him wait outside?"

"He didn't want to come in." Gorky said, lighting his second cigarette of the day, checking around for cameras one last time. As he inhaled, he could feel the insides of his lungs turning to crystal glass.

The maître d', hesitated, damming up his thoughts one last time before tapping his pen on the podium. His thoughts began to pour out of his brain down through the roof of his mouth, collecting in a pool between them.

"She didn't come in today."

"What did he want to talk to her about?"

"He didn't say. He was unhappy, though."

"How would you know?"

"It's in the eyes mostly. And the shoulders. In your line of work, I'm sure you see it all the time, non? A man who wraps himself tight, making sure the world does not get too much of him. I see it all the time."

"What is it about his eyes that makes you think he's sad?"

A large man with a flat, broad nose approached the podium, placing a clear glass cup of steaming liquid on the podium and disappearing back into the dark.

"It's always the same." Said the maître d', unwrapping the cigarette he had taken and dropping it into the liquid, paper and all. "They shine back at you, the eyes I mean, like they can't take all the light in on their own. I always imagine that if you could stick a flashlight behind them you could project what they're sad about on the wall. Work, strata, love, like a film."

The liquid began to bubble slightly as the salt diffused into the mixture, turning the drink a light effervescent blue.

"Do you like films, detective?"

Gorky watched the bubbles drift up along the sides of the glass, giving off a gentle fizz as they reached the surface. Inside he could feel his rib cage expanding.

"I do." He replied, trying to remember the last time anyone had asked him a personal question on the job.

"A man like you deserves a break from time to time, don't you agree?"

Gorky took another drag from his cigarette, holding the smoke in the back of his throat and stuffing it down inside him. The two sat in silence as Gorky turned the question over in his mind.

"A break from what?" He replied, finally letting the smoke out.

Gorky's eyes were twin volcanoes in the dark, magma leaking from the edges, streaming down his face. The maître d' sighed loudly, allowing a smirk to form across his face.

"Perhaps I'm wrong."

Gorky nodded and turned to leave, catching his reflection in the empty window. The blood that flowed from his eyes was thick and sticky on his face, a single drop managing to fall to his collar. He wiped his eyelashes clean with a handkerchief and replaced his sunglasses, watching as the maître d's reflection drained the tobacco-speckled drink in a single gulp.

Outside, Jean-Baptiste was gone, disappeared along with the car they arrived in. Staring at the abandoned storefront across from the Jade Mountain, Gorky wondered what would be projected on the wall if he could shine a light behind his eyes. His mind stopped briefly on a snowy pier, ships moored in ice on the horizon, a sad, hopeful smile slowly melting away in the pre-dawn dark, but was quickly replaced by a steady wash of violet-tinged blood dripping down the vacant windows.

Chapter 12

Detective Gorky's hard rubber soles squeaked against the freshly polished floor of the Department of Records and Retention as he made his way toward the Uptown rail station. His thoughts lingered on the face of Viviana Mendes. Her eyes had tucked in around the edges as he spoke about Henry, her molars making a soft grinding noise that felt as faint and delicate as the scent of her perfume, almost subliminal. She was worried, but she seemed far from concerned, a strange combination that led her to dig her ruby nails into her arm, slipping them just beneath the skin, concealing the scene beneath her desk.

The train pulled into the empty platform with a long hydraulic cough, the doors swinging open to a vacant railcar. Gorky tucked himself into the seat beneath the corner camera, feeling slightly invisible, like a transparent man with a dotted outline. The screens flickered on, picking up the feed of a documentary already in progress as the rail began to hum beneath him. Strange drawn-out shots of skinless men carved from lavastone surrounded by banana trees, their muscles and teeth peeled back and visible to the plants. The narrator's voice cut softly through the canopy noise, her distant tone like someone reading an eye exam.

"His flayed skin is a sign of fertility in the coming months, the extra hand of his victim proof of the valley's plentiful harvest."

Images of a man having his ears removed made Gorky's squirm in his seat, the steady stream of blood and the sound of tearing, like thick paper, making him pick beneath his nails nervously. He tried to look away as the man had the skin peeled from his back in long, smooth sheets, but the image was impossible to escape, projected on every surface. As the man's spine was revealed, Gorky could feel the skin peeling back on his hands from the fingertips down. Looking at his pale digits, he wondered what color lay beneath the surface of his skin, a sticky blackish-red like port wine the only color he could conjure.

Without warning, the train screeched to a halt, the images flickering on and off as the narrator's voice cut in sporadically, her distant tone sounding as if it had been recorded in a perfectly sealed concrete box. The screens clicked off, leaving the car aglow in blue static. The image of the obelisks still towered over Gorky in the dark, the sparks and hisses of the car as ancient and mysterious as a distant jungle canopy.

An image of the railcar having its exterior pulled away, like a second skin, manifested in his head. He felt secure, sure of the vitality of the Metropol. He would feast for decades, everyone in the city would, so long as everything stayed exactly as it was in that moment.

The walls felt as though they were constricting, like drying leather on a sun-stained pole. Gorky pulled the emergency exit and pried the door open with his short fingernails, cutting himself just along the nail bed of his ring and middle finger. Outside, the skyscrapers and street lights flickered and skipped, the dark void below the elevated rail stuttering in and out of existence. Gorky grabbed the service rail and stepped onto the thin wire catwalk toward the next station, leaving the discarded husk behind as he wandered toward Henry's apartment. As the lights failed around him, Gorky felt the heat coming off the city, all the stored power evaporating into the night sky. Each time the lights tried to start, the sound of generators and neon deafened him, shocking him back to reality from his floating world of darkness on the high wire.

The Metropol wheezed through its dying routine, the sound of the generator's discharging power coming in like wind blowing through a long forgotten cave. At the next station Gorky stepped down from the rail, his form cutting the evening in two as he moved through the streets, the whole of the universe dividing on either side of him. The stars above were an endless void pulling light up, and as he stared up into them, he could feel the dark looking down at him. Confident the cameras were busy watching the world fail, Gorky struck a thin stick match against a nearby brick wall and lit another cigarette. The flame differentiated himself from the night, he thought. A beacon of civilization, blue smoke pouring from his nose, salt crystals forming at the edges of his lips. He picked them off and climbed the stairs to Henry's apartment.

This had been the third power failure this year, but it could have been the three hundredth and nothing would have changed, Gorky thought to himself. Looking over the courtyard, he watched the city settle into place, everyone stopping their tasks and moving inside, abandoning the streets.

As Gorky inhaled, the blue tip of his cigarette illuminated his face dimly. He sat at the edge of the bed and reached into his pocket, producing a series of photographs of Henry's room. Gorky inspected them closely, the depth of his vision penetrating the darkness, the patterns in the walls lining up with the pictures in his hands. He tried to focus on the differences, the discrepancies between what was and what was not there forming an image of Henry in his mind. Missing Winter coat, towels gone, pantry empty, his mind pausing as he noticed a small piece of paper missing from Henry's desk.

Gorky leaned close over the picture, his right eye inches from the scene, his brain picking out the letters on the paper as they came without order, arranging themselves in his mind: "Come Join Us."

He inspected the travel zone poster and tried his best to ignore the voice that told him to go to the mirror, to stare into his leaking blue eyes. The leg work was over. Gorky knew where he was going, at least superficially. A single breath escaped from deep within Gorky's lungs as he fell back on Henry's bed and closed his eyes, letting the terrible electric high rip through his veins, his body convulsing in the dark, fading into the night.

Chapter 13

The following morning's sun rose across the city skyline like a guillotine. Detective Gorky rubbed the back of his neck as he stepped down the stairs, the whole city blinking in mechanical operation all around him. Walking along the industrial parkway roads that stretched the twenty blocks between Henry's apartment and the station, Gorky kept his mind occupied by counting cars and people that passed before stepping into a fast dinery across from the precinct station.

Inside, Jean-Baptiste hovered above his seat at the counter, retying his ponytail and watching the waitress who floated uncomfortably around the edges of the bar. Gorky sat down next to Jean-Baptiste and watched the waitress move toward him cautiously, taking his order from a good five feet away. In her off-white outfit and her long graying hair, she reminded Gorky of a moth trapped in a light fixture. He ordered a warm ration plate and a hot cup of Pero before settling into his seat and pushing his glasses back up his nose.

"Any luck last night?" Jean-Baptiste asked, sipping a cup of genuine coffee and letting the smell waft down to Gorky.

"I've got everything we need."

"Where are we headed?"

"The Elk Range, out in the Third Wilderness Zone."

Jean-Baptiste inhaled sharply through his large nose and held it in.

"What's he want there?"

"I don't know." Gorky paused as the waitress delivered his meal and shuffled away backwards. "But I suspect he doesn't want anything, other than to not be here."

Jean-Baptiste's face was sunken and somber, his vision hovering in the distance between the kitchen and the counter. He looked as if he were glowing at the edges slightly.

"Do you think he'll be alive when we find him?"

"It's hard to say. There's a lot of winter left." Gorky said, letting the Pero burn his upper lip.

"When do we leave?"

"Twenty minutes and I'll be ready. Does that give you enough time?"

Jean-Baptiste opened his coat and revealed a smooth silver revolver tucked against his chest. Gorky nodded and went to work on the square block of food placed in front of him, cutting it into smaller squares and eating his way around the perimeter until only a single bite was left. He let the thick, slightly metallic taste coat his tongue before washing it off with the rich, deeply burnt taste of his Pero.

"Hey." Jean-Baptiste began in a tone that showed something similar to concern. "You okay to drive?"

Gorky finished his drink and slid his sunglasses down his nose, revealing a pair of pale blue eyes glowing around the edges, the capillaries burst in random, caustic patterns across the white marbles. Jean-Baptiste's smile brought Gorky back to a New Year's party from many years before, that same wide, satisfied grin spread across a pair of pink lips, an image he had held onto for a long, long time. Jean-Baptiste threw Gorky the keys and stepped out of the way, letting him make his way to the steering wheel, his blood phosphorescent and humming like an electric cable dangling from a broken pole.

Chapter 14

The expressway out of town was as deserted as ever, the large off-road monstrosity rumbling in a straight line while Gorky tapped at the wheel with his fingers, one hundred miles-per-hour of unstoppable calamity. Inside the car, the banging of the motor hushed into steady vibrations that tickled Jean-Baptiste's ankles as he leaned back and rested his feet on the dashboard. As he watched the scenery passing from the corner of his eye, he lingered on the redline that cut between the unkempt wilderness and the edge of the city. The long strip of sulfured earth burnt away at the edges of the vines, splitting the Metropol away from the world, keeping everything else at bay.

"He should have just run into no man's land." Jean-Baptiste closed one eye and held his fingers out at the woods, loading the chamber of his imaginary gun and clicking his tongue. "We'd already be done."

"It'll be good to get out to the border zones." Gorky said, barely listening at all. His fingers kept up their frantic pace as he continued to count up to fifty over and over in his mind.

"Why?" Jean-Baptiste asked, pulling his seat up.

Gorky didn't respond, his mind skipping as he started back at one.

The road shot straight through the wild for twenty miles of strange and dangerous woods before spilling out into the gentle sloping hills of the fuel yards. The woods disappeared gradually before giving way to the deep rust hills, coal seams and charcoal farms dotting the swelling expanse. The chemical processing sheds bellowed out the softest shade of blue-gray ash that stuck to the surface of the earth like spray paint. The overall effect was that of a frozen sea, storm winds swelling and turning the water into icy peaks and deep valleys. The air that leaked in through the vents smelled like strawberries and kerosene, the former coming from the strange mix of chemicals that collected in pools at the base of the hills.

Jean-Baptiste barely noticed the shift in scenery, his mind lingering on all the work still left to be done.

"I don't see why we have to do this." Jean-Baptiste offered in a voice coming from a far-off place, the sound projecting from deep in his body.

Gorky stopped counting, focusing his attention back into his body.

"Why we have to kill him?"

Jean-Baptiste raised an eyebrow and looked over at his driver.

"Why we have to come out here to do it. Five days out here and he's dead of exposure. We could be back at the office, or on the streets at least."

"Any system needs rules to exist. You can't let someone break the rules and get away with it. If we let that happen, the whole system would collapse."

"Bullshit." Jean-Baptiste said, rubbing his eyes. His mind was as smooth and gray as the hills they wound through, not focusing on a single thought for more than a second.

"The system only works if people believe it works. If they can just leave, then how does it function?"

Jean-Baptiste stayed quiet for a long time. The hum of the engine sunk him deep in his seat, his lungs expanding and contracting like a bellows to the sound of the road.

"I was with a girl, it was after we got tea the other night, remember? Long eyelashes, small ears, skin so soft you thought you might tear it if you pushed too hard. Like you could fall right through her."

"I don't need to hear about who you're sleeping with."

"We're driving on the outskirts, and she asks me what I do. And I tell her exactly what it is I do to stay Upstrata. Well, usually they get a bit jumpy when I talk about work, but I do it anyway. It worries them, they tense up. You can almost see the outlines of their skeletons they get so tight, well usually. Not her, though. She asked me to describe it. And you know what I said?"

Gorky stayed silent, waiting for Jean-Baptiste to continue on his own.

"I described what we did last winter in that cabin two miles from the redline. You remember?"

"What you did." Gorky snapped back quickly. The conversation suffocated between the two.

"Is that how you see this?" Jean-Baptiste said, fixing his hair in the rear-view mirror. "We did. I may have been holding the knife and the bucket, but you stood in the doorway watching. If you've got any kind of part in the collection, you get credit, right? So how'd we find the cabin? How'd I know where to wait?"

"Say what you want, there's a difference in what we do."

"Are you telling me that if that sorry loser had turned the tables and cut my throat, you would have what? Let him go?"

Gorky settled into the scenario. He imagined Jean-Baptiste's throat splitting end to end, the skin falling off his partner's muscles in ribbons, peeling back across his body. Gorky didn't have an answer.

"Well, anyway, I'm describing it to her, and she's got these shades on, blue and red lenses, and she keeps rubbing her legs, so I pull over thinking she's a real freak. Like way out there sexually. I'm thinking I hit the jackpot, but it turns out she's wiping sweat from her palms, and when I reach over and take her shades off, she's crying."

"Is there a point to this story, or are you just telling me about the last time you made your date cry?"

"She doesn't say anything for a long time, and then we start going at it in the car. Real lifeless sex."

"Are you done?"

"And that's when she asks me to kill her."

The mid-winter sun dipped behind a tall plume of smoke that rose from the Western-front, leaving the hills cast in dark blue shadows. The road was checkered with patches of darkness that sucked up the light and consumed it, the way apes consume small monkeys, the way caves consume the wind. Jean-Baptiste relished the long silence that descended on them.

"What did you do?" Gorky asked, his voice soft and delicate, barely wanting to know the answer.

"We finished having sex, I took her to the redline, and watched as she stepped over the boundary. And that's when I shot her in the back of the head."

The inevitability of the sentence fell like a guillotine.

"Brains came out of her eyes, barely any blood, though. Like she was a robot or something. Never seen a person with so little blood."

Gorky's mind was completely blank. No new ideas rose to the surface as they barreled down the road.

"Well, my credit score comes in two days later, so yesterday, and how many points did I lose? Go on and guess." Gorky bit his cheek, not wanting to guess.

"One point. One fucking point in morality. How do you like that? She was worth one point. She was a good one, too. Seemed real Upstrata. Imagine what I'd get for killing some low life? Do four sub-twenty-fives make one Upstrata? If so, I could take out four a quarter and make up the difference by going to church, don't you think?"

"So?"

"What do you mean 'so'?"

"I mean what's your point? Or is this just a story about the last woman you killed?"

"My point is that I don't see why we have to follow this guy all the way out into the goddamned mountains to retrieve his frozen corpse. Why do we have to do all this work for one stiff? So what if he broke the rules? Why should I have to be here because of that? He'll die whether we do our job or not, and what's the punishment for failing? A point? The juice doesn't seem worth the squeeze on this one."

"You sound like a revolutionary."

Jean-Baptiste laughed through his nose, rubbing his hands over his face to feel the rough skin scraping against his eyes and cheeks.

"I don't want the system to fail. It suits me just fine."

"Except for right now."

"I just don't get why it's so important we get him."

Gorky weaved the machine around the darkest corners of the road, just barely keeping himself between the imaginary lane in the center of the road.

"You can get away with most anything, so long as you know the rules of the game. The one thing you can't do is flip the board and quit. Quitting means you're not engaged, you're not contributing, and soon enough it means you'll be playing a new game with new rules that someone, maybe everyone, likes more. Maybe one in a hundred runners ghost out if we don't chase them. Give it a couple of years and you'll have a community. Give it a couple of decades and you'll have a town, then a city, and a state. Then it's war. So yeah, we have to find this guy, and you're going to kill him if he isn't already dead, because any system is better than nothing."

The car drifted back into the right lane, and the two sat quietly with nothing on their minds. Jean-Baptiste kept his eyes closed, the dim light illuminating his silhouette around the edges. He looked as if he wasn't a part of the world, as if he had been cut out and placed there against the deepening shades of gray that spread out into the distance.

"That wasn't the last woman I killed." Jean-Baptiste said, breaking the silence. "Pull over soon."

The two rode quietly to the next exit, the silence filling up the car like water. Even if he spoke, Gorky did not think anyone would be able to hear him.

Chapter 15

The car rolled to a stop at a service station positioned at the edge of the fuel yard. The tall steel-slatted fence that ran from horizon to horizon separated the natural world of trees and stones and clear-water springs from the engine of society. Gorky turned off the car and dropped the keys on the dashboard, his eyes locked on the white-capped mountains between the slats. It reminded him of old film stuck in a reel, the images caught between bars.

Jean-Baptiste stood outside the car, unzipping his fly and relieving himself in the dirt behind the car's rear tire.

"Is this the place?" He asked, staring at the ground.

"This is as far as he could have gotten legally. Cameras didn't pick him up coming or going, but he was on the bus at the previous stop and gone when it came back through, so it makes sense he got out here."

"Pretty good for a paper-pusher."

Gorky placed his hand on the hood of the car, pulling it away as it seared the skin on his outstretched fingers.

"Paper-pushers have all day to fantasize about disappearing. You spend five years imagining something, you'd expect to be ready when the time comes."

"That's why every kid is great at sex their first time." Jean-Baptiste laughed, zipping up his fly, kicking the gray dirt and leaning his elbow against the hood of the car. Gorky watched his partner's jacket smoke slightly at the sleeves but didn't bother to say anything about it.

As they looked out at the wilderness, a short, skinny man with large wet eyes and rice-paper skin came shuffling up to the car from the station, approaching the two with his hand behind his back. His muscles were wiry and tight as he ran his teeth along the inside of his cheek, biting softly. Gorky flashed his badge and motioned to the gas tank, watching as the old man placed the screwdriver he had been concealing into his pocket and shuffled off to the station.

"Would have shoved that thing right up his nose if he pulled it on me." Jean-Baptiste said, spitting.

"Well he didn't, so relax."

The man returned, dragging a wagon full of gasoline with a pump which he cranked to siphon the gas into their tank. Gorky looked at the oil stains that blotted the old man's body like a disease, a black, oozing pox that shined in what little light made it through the clouds. A smear beneath the man's left eye looked particularly infectious, ready to drip out and spread down his cheek at any moment.

"My map says the quickest way to get to Sopris is by going over McClure's Pass." Gorky said, still fixating on the oil.

"Storm coming down the hills tonight." The old man said, wiping his hands on a rag he kept on his belt loop.

"What kind of storm?" Jean-Baptiste asked as he moved around behind the man.

"Hard to say. Could be a fair bit of snow. Pass is gonna be hard, either way."

"You spend a lot of time out there?" Jean-Baptiste asked.

The old man shrugged, his shoulders rolling in their sockets like ball bearings.

"How would you get up there on foot?" Gorky asked, studying the land and checking it against his map.

"Up the gulch there's a way they used to take cows and horses when this was grazing land. That'd be quickest. Dangerous, but quick."

"How well traveled is it?"

"It isn't. Not anymore."

"Is that where he is?" Jean-Baptiste asked, turning to Gorky.

"It would explain how he got off the map. Doesn't explain where he learned about it, though."

Jean-Baptiste grabbed the man by his belt and yanked him backwards, sending him tumbling down onto the cold gray earth.

"Don't suppose you told him, did you?" Jean-Baptiste asked, spitting on the ground again.

The old man shook his head, his words choking and backing up in his throat, causing him to stammer heavily.

"If he goes up the gulch where does he come out?"

"Black Canyon." He said with a shake that rattled his teeth like a motor purring through the quiet dark.

Gorky traced his fingers over the hills, a stream of light forming after his fingertip as he imagined the path.

"So we're going to have to follow him up there?" Jean-Baptiste asked, watching Gorky's hand make an X in the air.

"No. We can wait on the other side. We'll get over the pass and double back around a couple of miles. There's only one way out of the gulch if the map's right."

"You got any coffee?" Jean-Baptiste said, pushing his heel into the old man's shoulder.

"Pero. We've got Pero."

"Shit. We'll take it. And anything else you've got to pass the time."

The old man ran off, disappearing into the unlit station.

"You think he told our ghost how to get through the mountains?"

"Maybe. I don't think so, though."

"I'm going to write him up, just in case."

Gorky got back into the car and rested his eyes. He imagined the twisting and turning path, the rocky crags and winding streams, and the deep, uncompromising silence that must have been out there in the wild. He imagined it like a giant cube, dense and impenetrable from the outside laying over the valley, cutting into the earth at odd angles. He wondered how they would get in as he faded in and out of consciousness, the salt finally rolling back as his blood crept to a slow, thick crawl.

PART IV:

THE TASTE OF PINE

Chapter 16

Henry's eyes opened slowly, left then right, the dull blue cloud-filtered light crashing over his sprawled-out body like waves in the mid-winter Atlantic. Straight up above his head, the tall rock face loomed, the top barely visible, slanting away in an almost imperceptible angle. As he shifted his weight a short, gripping pain squeezed his ribs, pulling him deeper into the ground. Henry's muscles shifted the cracked bones, trying to keep them in one place. He watched the sun move in phases behind the woolen blanket that draped over the waking world. All the bitter cold he could not feel shifted back and forth above him in the wind.

After watching the sun move a quarter of the way across the sky, when it was well past noon, Henry was able to roll over onto his right side before pushing himself onto his hands and knees. He felt the soft earth shift as he pushed into it, as if the whole world was moving away from him. The wet grass spread through his fingers like freshly cleaned hair as his hands were drawn deeper into the warm ground. Henry imagined a pool of water, his fingers slipping through the surface tension until his whole body was floating.

Looking around, he measured the circumference of green grass in every direction, a circle as wide as his old apartment sitting between the cliff face and a gently bubbling stream. At the edge of the circle, winter piled itself up, the snow slanting upward in a ramp, as if anything dropped in the distant wild would slowly roll down to this very spot. In the center of the circle stood a twisted apple tree with small misshapen fruit, red and yellow, hanging and leaning against the tree. Henry reached out toward the base of the tree, causing his ribs to make a sound like tissue paper crackling as he grabbed an apple and pulled it back toward himself.

After letting his head rest on the ground, waiting for the pain to subside, he took a small bite from the bitter apple and remembered the moments before the fall, his foot slipping on the wet hard clay, his line catching him, bouncing him up slightly, and then the feeling of weightlessness that coursed through his body. Every bone disintegrating, blood evaporating, skin shredding in ribbons until all that was left was the part of him that kept memories real and alive. He counted his possessions on the ground as he chewed, finding the strength to tug at his backpack after finishing the apple.

Henry gathered his meal bars, placed his journal in his backpack, and pulled the rope in, placing them in a pile with his thick winter coat. The air was only slightly crisp, a cool Fall day, and down closer to the earth a trace of Spring could be felt in the heat leaking up through the ground. Reading from a medical textbook which he considered to be his own now, Henry removed his shirt and wrapped a bandage around his chest. He diagnosed his symptoms as multiple cracked ribs, but as he finished the wrapping, he was uncertain how bad the injury was. Once the bandages were on, he felt better, except when he twisted or tried to inhale deeply or suddenly. Running would be out of the question, he thought, as he replaced his thermal shirt.

In all directions aspen trees poked through the fog, anchoring everything save for the damp outlines of the tallest mountains, their ghostly shadows appearing wet and transient in the distance, as if they might disappear or move when he wasn't looking. Henry leaned against the tree and ran his fingers through the Kelly green mat, the sound of the babbling brook calming him, slowing his heartbeat. He didn't want to think about the cold, or the wind, or the fog and what was in it. He closed his eyes and tried to ease the feeling of dread that kept itself alive in his heart, but he could not let it go. Not completely.

With his eyes closed, he felt like he was falling again, formless. The ground seemed nonexistent, the tree an illusion. His body floated through the vacuum of night, falling through the stars, strange constellations taking form around him, stretching out in every known direction. In his recovering dreams, Henry traced the outlines of ancient forms in the sky. The swarms of moths, the endless deluge of beetles, the line of cicadas encircling the world, all expanding out, stretching to leave their forms behind, eternally tracing the path toward the universe's expanding edge.

Chapter 17

Henry stirred to the pinprick needles of frost in his skin, ice crystals forming inward through his pores, barely cutting into his bloodstream. The tree he leaned against was petrified in the frost, as still and unyielding as if it had existed for millennia in that same spot. The ground around him was gently windswept, a wash of blue-gray snow drifting just above the surface of the earth. Henry crawled to his coat, the hard ground digging the crystals deeper into the sides of his hands. He wrapped himself in the stiff fabric and waited fruitlessly for it to warm him.

The wind whispered nonsense into Henry's ears as it rushed over him. He listened for patterns, waiting for something to become clear before giving up and gathering his belongings and scanning the horizon. He wouldn't try climbing the cliffside to get over the mountain that stood between him and an infinite wash of unprotected wilderness.

There was only one option, he had to go around. The light blue of the frozen grass disappeared beneath his boots as he made his way over the snowbank that encircled the tree, giving way to a perfect white that reflected all the light it could not catch back into the sky.

As he walked, Henry's mind wandered back to his no-doubt brutalized apartment, to the empty space that surely existed at his desk, and for a brief moment to Eva, who he had no reason to linger on, but chose to anyway. He thought of her walking in front of him, cutting the gentle wild, calming the storm before he set foot in it.

Henry let out a sudden scream as he reached the top of a small hill that sloped down around the edge of the mountain. His voice echoed off the rocks and careened down along the riverbank that led off to the south. He watched as two images tightened up in the distance, a pair of big horned sheep stopping to observe him for a moment before making their way up the mountain's steep edge. Henry watched as they climbed, his hand grasping at his ribs as he wondered if anyone he ever knew would have an opportunity to stand in the middle of nowhere and scream. He considered the significance, what he could tell others that only he knew. There was a feeling of importance that sunk Henry into the snow, the pressure settling down and nesting over him like a large fat crow. He felt like a seer, yelling prophecies to an unlistening crowd.

As he continued on, Henry's thoughts flipped back to the teahouse, his mind resettling on Eva and shaking free like a snow globe, the image of her coming through as the snow settled. Each time she appeared in his mind, he counted the ways in which the woman he imagined failed to exist. She was a fantasy, a person stolen from time, a memory detached from any real form. Tea-giving deity, fountain of kindness, hallmarks of an oil painting more than of a living person. But as he continued around the cliffside, his neck tilted back looking for a way to ascend, he decided to keep his fantasy alive. He would never see her again. He would never rejoin society, It was not an option. It was only fair, he thought, to take a token from the mechanical world, a false memory of a person he could have loved, rather than just infatuated over, if he had the time. If she had never changed.

In the opaque middle-distance Henry watched as the harsh slope slowly broke away, grading down into a walkable path. He put his head down to avoid the wind and continued with purpose. On the other side of the mountain was a valley he would follow to the base of the Elk Mountains. It would be a long walk, ten days of falling through a cold he had never experienced in the city, his very bones growing brittle, hairline fractures forming along his shins. But once he was through the mountains, beyond the wilderness park and down the other side, he would be unquestionably free.

The path led up in a long curve, tracing the outline of the mountain in what felt like a perfect circle. If he could float above the peaks of every small mountain, Henry imagined he could draw a circle around each one, the whole of nature breaking down into circles and the spaces between circles, dots to form constellations on the earth.

Henry continued through the afternoon, the sun's diffused light like an hourglass draining down across the sky to a cold he would not survive without shelter. He weaved his way through the pine trees on the path, stopping to pick up any loose branches that sat beneath the canopy, tucking their hard exteriors beneath his left arm. As he ascended Henry could feel the ground firming up beneath his boots, flattening out, becoming smoother and smoother until it was clear that this had, at one point, been a road. A paced out walkway lost to time and the elements, eroding into a faint reflection of what it had once been. As he felt his boots click hard against the earth, Henry looked down to find broken pieces of concrete waiting in his boot tracks, the pale gray bringing his mind back to the Metropol.

Henry thought of his apartment's courtyard. He imagined a reality where everyone had suddenly dropped, their cold bodies fertilizer for the slow encroachment of the city's exotic courtyard plants, the day lilies and ornamental trees realizing their opportunity and spreading out, eroding the world left behind. Then, two hundred years later, he would return. The buildings crumbled, the skeletons turned to mulch, the concrete torn to pebbles by dandelion roots. This gave Henry a soft comfort as he ducked beneath a thick cluster of trees, coming out on the other side to the skeleton remains of a stone cottage in an overgrown clearing.

Henry approached the worn facade, stepping through the empty door frame and standing in the snow-filled remains, looking up through the open roof. He placed his bag down on a pile of wood that had once been a shelf and began to shovel the snow from the building one handful at a time, excavating small hidden things. A metal fork, a knife, the remains of a book's rotted cover. He was an archeologist in the tundra, his frostbitten fingers doing the delicate, thankless work of digging out the remains of an unknown people.

After an hour or so of constant shoveling, a half-eaten broom revealed itself in the snowpack. Henry swept away the remaining snow, pushing it out the door and excavating a livable cottage, the remnants of another living human revealing themselves in the organization of the single room. A figure sitting by the fire, writing down their thoughts, fur traps set for the following day. Not quite happy, lonely but content. A ghost leaving static traces through the last great memory left on the mountain.

Chapter 18

The smoke rose up from the campfire in the center of the cottage through the blankets Henry had hung as a roof, the small hole in the middle where they intersected allowing the smoke to pull through into the night. Lying against his bag, he placed the rusted kitchen knife in the fire hoping to clean off the dull blade. He flipped through his copy of *The Wonders of Instinct* that he had bookmarked by folding the corner over, reading through the section on cicadas where he had left off.

His mind wandered with the smoke up through the tent into the well-set sky, the stars and clouds looking as still as glass. Something could be heard moving around the cabin, but it didn't bother Henry. He had stacked the furniture by the open doorway, locking himself into his cell. The night was cautious and still outside his fortified walls, things barely stirring, moving with slow, nervous energy. One hundred years of poisoning the land at the edge of the Metropol had left things anemic in the wild, toxic to the marrow. The dust settled down and passed through the generations, putrefying everything in painful throws that would last for centuries. He wondered if humans had lived through the same ordeal, but could not say. No one talked about it, or taught it much, just that it happened and that the world was like the Metropol only in the good places.

Henry pulled the red-hot blade from the fire with a stick, letting it cool and sputter against the ground before picking it up and holding it up above his head, listening to the soft hiss the oxidized metal gave off against the cool air. The cabin was warming slowly, the fire spreading up his toes and into his knees, ready to ignite his body given proper time. Henry waited patiently, placing another broken branch in the pit and watching as it splintered at the edges. After the blade had cooled down to a silvery hue he placed it in the dirt and reached for his journal. Henry tapped his forehead with his pen before beginning, allowing the thoughts to leak out the front of his skull and drip onto the page.

When he first started journaling, he couldn't pinpoint his motivation. But as he filled the pages, he came to understand himself a bit more. Three years ago, he could not imagine being the man he had turned into, lying in the dirt completely alone. Looking back, he could not recognize the man he was or understand why he had chosen to live his life the way he had for so many empty years. So this, he told himself, would be the best way forward. A way to get to know himself, to understand the man who would lead him to who he would become.

He wrote about his day's travels, of the sheep and the river, and the clearing and the apples he had packed in his bag. He asked himself questions and tried to write the answers as best he could.

How do you feel?

Tired. Excited. Cold, but getting warmer.

Where are you going?

Somewhere safe, I hope.

Then he wrote down thoughts that freely leaked from his mind, notes on his readings that he felt would be important to remember.

When cicadas come out in the summer, they don't choose to come out all at once. If they don't, they miss their chance to reproduce, to keep things moving forward, and so they all have to come out together biologically. It's as compulsive as wanting water, or sleep, subliminal like breathing.

Lying here feels new. Like I haven't done it before.

After writing his thoughts he placed his journal on the ground and rummaged through his bag for a meal bar and the maps he had taken from work, stretching them across his knees and trying to find his exact location. He chewed on the rubbery, nutrient dense square as he traced his finger over the wilderness, drawing circles around the mountains in the firelight. It would take him as far as the foothills of the Elk Mountains, and then everything would be a mystery, for him and everyone else. After folding the map, he leaned against his pack and tried to sleep, but something hummed out in the cold, ratcheting up in the dark, a buzz that moved the static around Henry's head. He remembered the last summer he spent as a child, the feeling of possibility before him, and the glow of the sun that made his skin medicine, warm and soothing to the touch.

Chapter 19

Henry's boots slammed against the frost-stained fields just outside the fuel yard as the sun pulled down on the horizon, leaving a small knife edge sliver of orange pushing through the mountains. As dusk began to settle in, he looked back over his shoulder at the fill up station burning in the dark, the electric lights the brightest sight for a hundred miles as the sun finally disappeared. He thought that if he could get far enough away, far enough that the light would disappear, he would feel something. His limbs were dead branches swinging at his sides, his organs dug out, leaving a hollow shell racing across the expanse, certain it would not make it further than the edge of the woods. He felt his soul escaping in flecks through his hurried, dry breath as he turned over his shoulder again and again, the light barely fading, always hovering just behind him.

Thinking back on his panicked rush toward the wilderness, Henry ran his fingers along his gums, remembering the pressure that built up beneath them as he ran, as if blood was going to spout out and pop his teeth like champagne corks. As his fingers reached the back of his molars, he felt that the pressure was still there, waiting to be let out, his gums achy and swollen, his teeth grinding together to try and counter the slow rotting sensation that made them feel loose. The path down the valley flattened out through the morning, small thin slabs of worn-down concrete taking shape among the loose dirt. As he descended the hillside the knot at the center of Henry's back slowly curled in on itself, pulling his sides and the tops of his shoulders back, tilting his chin up to the breaking blue sky.

Down where the path met the valley's base, Henry inspected the rusted steel that jutted out of the small icy river. The burnt orange bones of a once-strong bridge reached up from the frozen surface, water expanding out into puddles and pulling back where the metal stuck out and the ice could not form. He followed the river with his eyes as it wound into a small cave, the sound of falling water whispering softly across the barren sweep.

Henry's head brushed against the low branches of a pine tree with long, winter-stiff needles the shade of cooked spinach. He paused as the pointed tips gently cut against his scalp, picking a bunch and kneeling down at the edge of the river. He wiped the wispy layer of snow away from the ice and looked down at his warped reflection, noting how all the heat seemed to disappear close to the ground.

Smiling with his teeth out wide, he slowly slipped the first needle between his gums on the upper right-hand side, the pine sliding in at the edge of his teeth, sticking slightly as he rocked the needle back and forth until a warming sensation began to creep across his tongue. The needle began to move smoothly as he continued to work it around the tooth, the dark red of his blood pooling beneath his tongue and leaking out of the corner of his mouth. Henry opened wide and let a long thin stream of blood and saliva slide onto the ice below, sticking to the tacky surface. He repeated the process with his left-hand side, working his way inward and replacing the needles as they became soft and heavy with blood before placing a fresh needle up through the space between his two front teeth.

As he pulled the needle loose, a dam burst from his mouth, deep amber blood streaming in one large ribbon from his skull. He watched the warm sludge spill on the ice, as if someone had turned on a faucet in the back of his head. He reached for the handle behind him, coming up only with his hair. His tongue pressed against the roof of his mouth, accelerating the stream as he rocked the tip up and down along the back of his teeth.

Watching as the blood slowly turned brighter, trading the dark auburns for a light, bright crimson, Henry wondered how much blood he was losing. The world constricted around the edges, the wide mouth of the cave fading from Henry's vision. His blood looked pink, the ice dull and gray against its vibrant shades. Small blue flecks sparkled in the river, the roots of trees appearing like gold veins in the frozen dirt around him. Henry's frozen fingers traced the complex waterways that fed the pines. He leaned back as the bleeding came to a trickle, letting a little bit of pink blood fall back into his throat. The blood on his teeth had cooled and hardened now, leaving a smooth, refreshing feeling in his mouth, as if he had been chewing mint leaves.

Looking around, everything washed out in sepia tones. The breaking clouds and the tall abstract trees cast monochrome shadows across the valley's floor. Henry watched golden lines cut through the atmosphere, moving slowly toward him. He stumbled to his feet as he watched the lines pass him by, stepping away as more appeared around him. Henry stood perfectly still for a moment, allowing one to pass right through his chest. He felt a push, a gentle breeze rocking him onto his heels before he plunged into the water, his hands still clutching a single bloody pine needle.

No light broke in beneath the ice. No current pushed him along. Henry floated, turning slowly, the small blue flecks of ice like stars in the deep dark, no way of knowing which way was up.

PART IV:

A QUIET KIND OF SCREAMING

Chapter 20

"Missed." Gorky said, striking a match against the heel of his boot and lighting a cigarette that he held between his teeth.

"Shut up." Jean-Baptiste whispered, taking the butt of his pistol and placing it over his outstretched forearm.

The two stood silently, Gorky holding down the smoke and Jean-Baptiste exhaling slowly as he let off three more shots down into the canyon.

"There." Jean-Baptiste said, watching the body tumble into the icy river.

Gorky's heart sputtered and convulsed as he let the smoke pour out over his eyes from the roof of his mouth, layering the canyon in a pale white filter. He gasped for fresh air, but the thick smoke lingered around his mouth, causing him to spit and shake, his hands grasping for something he could not quite explain, something like a bag of fresh blood to pump into his system.

Jean-Baptiste holstered his gun and shook his head slowly, watching Gorky fumble for even footing on the steep, slippery rocks.

"You'll be dead by sundown." He said, shrugging and leaning against the cleanest rock he could find.

"I'll be fine." Gorky managed to wheeze out, a small trickle of blood flowing from his right eye, dripping electric blue on the cold red dirt.

"Your blood's toxic. What should I put in the report? Suicide?" Jean-Baptiste shook his head. "No. I'll say you drowned. I tried to save you, but the current carried you under."

Gorky didn't respond, letting the worst of the drug kick through him, sinking its hooks in behind his eyes and pulling his face inwards, intense pressure building around his nose and eyebrows. He knew he had gone too far this time, but deep in the woods, no one who cared would see him disintegrating.

"Let's pack up and go." Jean-Baptiste said as he walked past Gorky, his sleeve catching and pulling back as Gorky tugged on his long winter coat.

"We need the body." Gorky pulled the words in and readjusted his sunglasses as the cool, even part of the high that flattened out the mountains and made everything simple finally took over.

"He's dead." Jean-Baptiste said, trying to pull his sleeve away.

"We need to have a condition on the final report. We have to see the body." Gorky replied, letting the coarse navy wool scratch against his fingertips.

"Frostbitten. Hole in chest. Very dead."

A harsh wind rushed over the two men, swaying them both in place as they braced against the cold.

"Then it won't be hard to find him and make our report."

"Who cares what his corpse looks like? I'm not going down there. No one's watching, no one cares."

"We're watching each other." Gorky said, turning his head up to his partner.

Jean-Baptiste placed the barrel of his gun against Gorky's forearm and pulled the trigger, sending small pieces of skin and meat flying into the ground. The deep crimson blood in Gorky's arms emptied out quickly, his heart pumping new, freshly salted blood into the cool air, the red fading to a purple slurry and then, finally, giving way to electric blue.

Gorky's hand stayed clasped to Jean-Baptist's coat, unmoving.

"You can't feel a thing, can you?"

"It hurt plenty." Gorky replied.

Jean-Baptiste shook his head, a smile growing at the edge of his lips, laughter escaping despite his inner protest.

"Stop touching me and I'll go."

Gorky let his arm fall to his side as the two set off down the mountainside toward the river, a trail of blue marking their slow descent toward the rusted steel bridge.

Chapter 21

Jean-Baptiste snaked ahead of Gorky by ten even paces, the soles of his shiny red leather shoes echoing off the damp rocks and scratching at the soft cave walls as they descended the uneven slope. The cave's path curved down and around the slowly eroding rocks and boulders, a gentle trickle of water cutting a pathway into the ground for the two to traverse. Gorky looked back up at the cave's entrance and listened for the sound of the river branching off somewhere in the distance, obscured by darkness.

As they walked, their footsteps deepened, pulsing out from the cave floor and bouncing off every surface, pulling back towards the center and crashing against Gorky.

"What the hell is this stuff?" Jean-Baptiste asked, scraping away at the light purple glow that coated the water's edge with his heel.

"Bacteria." Gorky said, watching the blood drip from his arm and into the water, its salt-laden glow allowing him to track it around the nearest bend.

"*Bacteria.*" Jean-Baptiste said in Gorky's voice. "*Go down and find his body, don't shoot him in the head.* All these goddamn rules and look at yourself. You can't even stand straight."

Gorky leaned forward to continue on, feeling his toe catch on a rock as he crashed into the thin stream. He kept a soft focus on his blood in the water, casting a purple hue on Jean-Baptiste's shoes as they slid backwards into the dark.

"You act so fucking smart, but which of us is doing a better job? I killed a man today. All you've done is point and complain."

Gorky pushed himself off the ground and stumbled forward, Jean-Baptiste's eyes and teeth reconstituting in the dark, the rest of him remaining immaterial.

"If you were alone, you would have given up a long time ago. Without me you'd still be a beat cop handing out social credit violations."

"But I'm not alone." Jean-Baptiste whispered, the tunnel widening and coming into focus as the cave opened around him to reveal a cavern lit by holes in the collapsed roof above.

Light crossed in between torrents of water that fell through the open roof, the sound filling every inch of Gorky's skull, pushing out from the inside, ready to pop. The space stretched out and away from them, the barely lit dark unfathomable in its scope. Mist gathered like clouds high above them, water condensing and pouring down the walls into the vast lake that formed at their feet, water barely brushing the toes of Jean-Baptiste's shoes. Looking out at the dappled light that crossed over the surface of the inland ocean, Gorky traced the outlines of trees rising from the water, their scaled trunks and palm-like fronds dripping heavy with dew.

"Down there." Jean-Baptiste said, motioning to the pale purple rocks and fallen trees that sat just above the surface of the pitch-black water, winding their way across the dark like rope bridges stretched across a deep, unknown canyon. Down near the base of a distant tree, Gorky spotted something slumped over, shaking softly.

Jean-Baptiste took a careful step onto a nearby rock, lifting himself over its smooth surface and transferring his weight onto a nearby tree, slowly letting the entirety of himself rest on the scaly bark. The two walked across the rocks and crept along the fallen branches and tree trunks toward the figure in the distance.

Down below them, the water shimmered slightly, a surface like onyx broken only by the pale purple light of the bacteria that clung to life along the rocks below the water's surface. As Jean-Baptiste stepped onto a branch, his heel dipped into the black liquid, sending ripples across the smooth clean surface. Gorky watched the large, bony plates of something churning in the deep, its milky white spine almost breaking the water's surface as it traced a patch around the branches and rocks. Gorky stepped carefully, his eyes locked on his feet, the whole world vibrating and turning beneath him.

The sound of water crashed against their ears, shaking them as they moved closer to the figure in the distance, its form blinking in and out of sight as they wound their way across the uneven path. As they drew closer to their destination, the form beneath the ancient tree began to take shape, body, arms, hair, blood leaching into the water, sliding effortlessly from Henry Chenille's hollowed out chest. The two men drew themselves up onto the rock that leaned against the base of the tree, finally standing close enough to touch their prey.

"You lucky son of a bitch." Jean-Baptiste said, stepping up to Henry and pushing his torn shirt to the side with the barrel of his gun, inspecting the deep holes in his chest. "How high is that drop?" He asked Gorky, looking up at the nearest waterfall that cascaded into the sea.

"I don't know." Gorky replied, trying to imagine how many of the Metropol's tallest buildings would fit comfortably beneath the caving dome, resting on the surface of the sea.

"Any one of these rocks could have killed you, and yet..." Jean-Baptiste tapped the barrel of his pistol on Henry's forehead twice. "Here you are."

Gorky watched as Henry's blood-stained teeth poked out from between his thin blue lips.

"Here I am." Henry managed to whisper, his eyes wandering the cold dark sweep of trees and rocks, feeling the bitter damp air entering through the holes in his gums and chest. He felt something creeping into his body, filling up the space that blood used to fill, small crystals forming like snowflakes in his veins.

"You know," Jean-Baptiste continued, following Henry's gaze into the darkness. "when I first read your report, I figured we'd have you strung up on a post in the city square by the next day. A few hours wasted catching some pencil pusher who couldn't handle another day licking boots, who didn't have the guts to just kill himself. Cause most of the time that's all I am, a suicide machine. People just use me as a way out. Cowards, too afraid to take any agency in their lives. But you, you're something different. You're a fucking moron."

The smile on Jean-Baptiste's face gave way to gritted teeth, his brow turning inwards, his shoulders shaking violently.

"You actually thought you could get away with it, didn't you? You thought I wouldn't catch you? That I wouldn't put a bullet right through you?" Jean-Baptiste dug his thumb into Henry's chest, his scream drowned out by the sound of water.

"Just finish him." Gorky called out, standing away from the two, barely able to hear a thing.

"Finish him? Like he's a fucking meal? You mean kill the man, right? *Kill him so I can go home and forget this happened*, right?"

"It's our job."

"Our job? I thought it was my job, unless you want to participate."

Henry reached out and grabbed Jean-Baptiste's wrist, trying to pull the thumb from his chest to no avail. Jean-Baptiste took the butt of his gun and smashed it against Henry's shoulder, causing his arm to fall limp at his side.

"Don't touch my coat. For all the time you wasted, I'm going to take a body part. We'll start with your ears, and if you survive that, we'll work our way down. Knowing how hard you've been to kill, I think we might even make it to your toes before you check out."

"That's enough." Gorky yelled over the sound of the water.

Jean-Baptiste pulled the knife from his shoulder holster and placed it against the upper cartilage of Henry's ear, letting it rest there for a moment before pulling down quickly.

Gorky's body began to move forward, his hands grabbing at Jean-Baptiste's collar and pulling him backwards onto the wet rocks.

"Enough!" He yelled, the sound weakening as it spread out like ripples in the water.

Jean-Baptiste spun onto his heels and drove his knife up into Gorky's left armpit, the two colliding violently, spinning around the edge of the rock. Gorky gripped onto the hand that held the knife in place, pulling away swiftly and pushing hard, sending his own body back onto the ground.

As Gorky fell away, fingertips digging into the rock's surface, Jean-Baptiste's heels rocked against the water's edge. He watched Gorky's blood flow freely down the smooth stone surface, circling the edge of the rock, flowing past his shoes before sinking into the onyx deep. Jean-Baptiste thought of his empty, clean desk, of the paperwork he would have to fill out, his breath becoming clear and even. As he lifted his foot to step up onto the rock's surface, he felt the world lurch forward,

Gorky disappearing from his sight as he slid waist-deep into the water, his shoe slipping on his partner's still-warm blood. In the moments before he realized he was in danger, Jean-Baptiste's mind focused only on the cold crispness of the water sliding into his shoes and the feeling of something primordial welling up inside him.

From up on the rock, Gorky watched something ancient open its bony jaws and dig them into Jean-Baptiste's side, pulling him chest-deep into the water. Even in his shock, though, with all of his pure red blood spilling into the mouth of the pale armored leviathan, he did not scream. A laugh of shock and disbelief tried to escape Jean-Baptiste's mouth as he resigned himself to his first true experience with bad luck, but all that came out was a wash of blood.

Chapter 22

Henry Chenille was no longer screaming. He couldn't feel anything at all, save for a cold numbness that had replaced his blood, something he thought of as the universe filling in the empty space inside himself.

Detective Gorky took his last cigarette and placed it between his lips, fumbling to find a lighter tucked away in his damp coat. He pulled himself onto his dead feet, standing just above Henry. The two listened to the sound of water churning and bubbling at the rock's edge, waiting for the sound to stop.

"There's no way you're getting me back to the Metropol." Henry said as Gorky swayed like a tree about to be felled.

"No. I don't think I am." Gorky replied, pulling the pristine, unused revolver from its holster and letting it dangle at his side.

"I wonder what it all meant. There was a clearing a few miles back. I should have just kept laying there. I could have just dreamt." Henry choked and coughed between breaths, unable to keep his lungs fully inflated.

"It probably didn't mean anything. We all erode eventually."

For the briefest moment, Henry mouthed the words to a poem he had heard in a past life, the round vowels almost puncturing the event horizon of his lips before falling back into his empty shell. It was something he had heard at a rail station, standing in the cold, though it seemed strange to come to him now. A memory he had not intended to form, broadcasting clearly through the static.

Gorky's pistol barely made a sound as the hammer came down, the room already full to bursting with noise, wet and thick. He hardly knew the gun went off, the only signs being the smell of freshly burnt powder and the hole in the universe where Henry Chenille used to be.

As he put his gun away, Gorky felt the blood under his arm, poisoned and rich, thick enough to clog a coffee filter. He stepped down onto the tree below, uncertain if he could make it back to his car. He wasn't sure what he would say, or do, or how he would process this day once it passed, but as he dragged his body across the rocks and toward the surface world, Gorky felt something stirring in his head. A quiet kind of screaming that never left his lips, just rattling around, peeling his eyelids back, keeping him from doing anything but move forward, trying his best not to collapse and be swallowed up in the thin, aqueous void beneath his feet.

Acknowledgements

First and foremost, I want to thank Sam for always allowing me time and space to write. You mean the world to me.

Thank you to Jerry for being my first reader and editor, cover art designer, and partner in moving the needle.

Thank you, Shane, for being an amazing editor.

Thank you, Camper, for always advancing the Boar.

The dual aspect of the Boar Lord is prominent in this piece. His sorcering hand guides us toward understanding. His knife hand cuts the path dangerously. May his influence continue to grow.

Serge Anatole Fedorowsky

is an author based in Denver, Colorado. He can be found screaming as his flesh comes off in ribbons. The wind is poison on his exposed muscles. His love of salt forms the beginning of a dangerous friendship. It litters his home, waiting to pull the moisture from his bones.